The Hidden Agenda
of Sigrid Sugden

The Hidden Agenda of Sigrid Sugden

Jill MacLean

Fitzhenry & Whiteside

Text copyright © 2013 Jill MacLean

Published in Canada by Fitzhenry & Whiteside, 195 Allstate Parkway, Markham, Ontario L3R 4T8

Published in the United States in 2013 by Fitzhenry & Whiteside, 311 Washington Street, Brighton, Massachusetts 02135

www.fitzhenry.ca   godwit@fitzhenry.ca

10 9 8 7 6 5 4 3 2

Library and Archives Canada Cataloguing in Publication
MacLean, Jill, author
      The hidden agenda of Sigrid Sugden / Jill MacLean.
ISBN 978-1-55455-279-5 (pbk.)
      I. Title.
PS8575.L415H53 2013   jC813'.6   C2013-904971-1

Publisher Cataloging-in-Publication Data (U.S.)
MacLean, Jill.
      The hidden agenda of Sigrid Sugden / Jill MacLean.
[240] p. : col. ill. ; cm.
Summary: Sigrid Sugden is a member of the school's tough group of girls - all experts at blackmail, extortion and bullying. When she has a change of heart and wants to be a better person, nobody is willing to give her a second chance. She then discovers that sometimes, you might find an ally in the most unlikely place.
ISBN-13: 9781554552795 (pbk.)
1. Friendship – Juvenile fiction. 2. Bullying – Juvenile fiction. 3. Teenage girls – Juvenile fiction. I. Title
[Fic] dc23   PZ7.M3354hi 2013

Fitzhenry & Whiteside acknowledges with thanks the Canada Council for the Arts, and the Ontario Arts Council for their support of our publishing program. We acknowledge the financial support of the Government of Canada through the Canada Book Fund (CBF) for our publishing activities.

 ONTARIO ARTS COUNCIL
CONSEIL DES ARTS DE L'ONTARIO
an Ontario government agency
un organisme du gouvernement de l'Ontario Canada Council   Conseil des Arts
for the Arts   du Canada

Cover and interior design by Daniel Choi
Cover images courtesy of Chris Mills and Shutterstock
Printed in Canada by Friesens

MIX
Paper from
responsible sources
FSC   FSC® C016245
www.fsc.org

Acknowledgements:

I am very grateful to the Department of Communities, Culture and Heritage of Nova Scotia for assisting me with an Arts Nova Scotia grant. The grant was both a vote of confidence in my work and a tangible support for the first draft of *The Hidden Agenda of Sigrid Sugden*.

✓✓✓

My faithful editor, Ann Featherstone, took the manuscript of this book into her capable hands and made it better. Much better! Thank you, Ann, for understanding what makes a good story, and—even more important—for knowing exactly how to implement the necessary changes.

My thanks to Christie Harkin at Fitzhenry & Whiteside, whose suggestions further improved *The Hidden Agenda of Sigrid Sugden*. Thank you, also, for finding the photo of three (three!) shrikes, and for your openness about the girl on the bicycle.

My gratitude to Chris Mills and his daughter, Maris, of Ketch Harbor, NS, for the photo on the lower half of the cover. It was fun working with you, Chris.

As always, thanks to my grandson, Stuart, for "techy" support.

Arts
NOVA SCOTIA
NOUVELLE-ÉCOSSE

For my granddaughter, Jessica

ONE

to terrify

"**S**how her the photo, Sigrid," Tate says.

My nerves tighten like they always do when Tate swings into action. Trying to hide my reluctance, I hold out my smartphone. The battery's near dead but the photo comes up anyway. Violet Dunston looks at it and wilts.

Tate smiles. When Tate smiles, her lips curve and her eyes stay empty. "You don't want it posted online, do you, Vi?"

The photo shows Vi shoplifting in the Dollar Store; she's tucking pink socks into her jacket pocket, looking as furtive as anyone can look. Poor Vi. She's in grade five and skinny with wispy brown hair, and she doesn't have one clue how to dress. Her top, for instance. If she didn't shoplift it, she was gypped.

"Answer the question, Vi," Mel says. She's the muscles of our group.

"Yeah, Vi," Tate says. "It'll only take Sigrid two secs to post it."

"Please don't," Vi quavers, her eyes swimming with tears.

Here I am, feeling sorry for her. *Don't let it show...*

"Twenty bucks and Sigrid will delete the photo," Tate says.

"Twenty bucks!" Vi lifts one hand to her mouth and starts chewing her fingernails. Nothing much left to chew by the looks of them.

"You're getting a deal," Tate says.

Tate's good at figuring how much she can wring out of kids. Knows her market, you could say.

Vi wipes a ragged piece of skin down her jeans. "I can't get the money until Monday."

"The girls' washroom. Five to nine."

Vi edges away from us, then makes a dash for the mall exit.

"Let's go," Tate says. "McDonald's for a bite of lunch, then we'll hit the stores."

So that's what we do and it's okay, I guess. But I'm glad when Tate wheedles a drive from Kenny Bugden after his shift ends at McDonald's. School's out by now, and I want to go home.

As we approach Fiddlers Cove, Tate says, "You can drop us at the wharf, Kenny."

"The wharf?" I say, dismayed.

"You heard me," Tate says.

You gotta watch Tate when she uses her quiet voice.

We almost never go to her place because her parents give a whole new meaning to *strict*. We don't go to Mel's because her father threw away the welcome mat after her mother died. We can't go to my place because it's Seal's day off.

So ten minutes later, me, Tate, and Mel are sitting on the wharf on upended plastic barrels that stink of fish. The fog's so thick you could open your mouth and drink it; the foghorn's bellow is deadened to a moan. It reminds me of the sound Avery Quinn made when we posted a photo of him picking his nose.

He only came up with half the money. Tate had warned him.

I swipe at the drops of water collecting on the sleeve of my yellow jacket, watching them join together in a little river that pools at my elbow.

Mel's chewing her way down a Mars bar. She's a Corkum from Long Bight and never has much to say for herself, depending on her fists to get the message across. Tate's the talker of our little group: short, wiry Tate Cody with her shiny black hair that waves to her shoulders.

You want to know what Prinny Murphy calls the three of us? The Shrikes.

Strike. Shriek. Shrike.

Tate says, smiling the way a cat smiles before it nails a sparrow, "Sigrid, your face is as long as Monday. What's your problem?"

"I'm fine. Cold, is all. Wish I had a sweater."

"You're such a wimp...Okay, there's two reasons why we're here. First, we gotta talk about Prinny Murphy. And second, there's a real good chance she'll turn up. She often comes to the wharf to help her dad mend his lobster traps."

Especially on a Friday afternoon, with school out for the weekend. I chew my lip, my ears straining to hear footsteps through the fog.

"Prinny's getting too big for them crappy sneakers she wears," Tate says. "Telling me on the school bus the other day—in front of all the kids—that she's through giving us money. If we let her get away with that, we're done. Might as well join the volleyball team."

Mel looks puzzled. "We're gonna play volleyball?"

Tate's the only person I know whose sigh sounds razor-sharp. "We're not going to play volleyball, Mel. We're here to work on our strategy. Our game plan."

Mel crumples the wrapper in her fist. "There's ways of fixing Prinny Murphy."

"It's not that simple," Tate says, "because she's got friends now. Her and Laice and Travis, they're tight as the Trinity. And if Travis Keating is on your tail, so's the whole hockey team. But Prinny's been a nice source of income the last while and we wants that to continue. Don't we?"

She's looking right at me; her eyes could strip the

scales off a codfish. I roll a couple of stones around with my toe. Prinny's been a nice source of income because we had photos of her ma drunk in a club with a guy who wasn't Prinny's father.

Hey, Prinny, pay up or they go online.

"Prinny's ma is sober these days," I say. "Maybe it's time to put the screws to someone else."

"And let her get away with it? Just because Mel's short on brains, Sigrid, don't act like you are. Prinny Murphy could bring us down."

"So we lose face. So what?"

"We're not gonna lose face—or money," Tate says. "Not in my lifetime."

Mel stands up, the plastic barrel rasping on the concrete. She's big and pig-ugly, which is likely an insult to a decent pig.

She says, "I needs a jacket. I'll be right back."

One of the fishermen keeps his oilskins in a little shack near the end of the wharf. Although Mel sometimes borrows the jacket, she's careful with it, and she always puts it back on its hook.

Right and *wrong* can be slippery.

She disappears into the fog. Tate's left foot is vibrating on the concrete. Sure sign she's irritated.

I clear my throat. "Maybe Prinny didn't mean it. About not paying us any more money."

"Shut up."

The cold seeps into my bones. I count the number of seconds between the foghorn's moans. Twelve. Who decided on that particular number? Why not eleven? Or thirteen?

Then we hear Mel speaking, her words muffled by the fog. "Lookit who's here—Tate, we got company."

Prinny...

Tate leaps to her feet. I follow hard on her heels.

We hurry past two longliners, their decks and cabins as wet as if it's been raining. Then the foghorn blares so loud that I only catch the tag-end of what Tate's saying.

"...now we got something better to do."

Prinny Murphy is standing there. Red jacket, damp ponytail, her face a mask of terror.

She's alone. We're between her and the road to the cove. So she's not just alone, she's trapped.

I know all about *trapped.*

Prinny's eyes dart from here to there. She whirls and sprints into the fog, heading for the end of the wharf where her father parks his truck and moors his speedboat.

Mel pounds after her, Tate on her heels. I race behind them, past piles of rope, a few lobster traps, an old killick lying on its side, and the whole way I'm praying Prinny's dad will be sitting on a fish barrel, mending his traps.

Tate yells, "No need to rush—Prinny ain't going nowheres." She laughs—a laugh that grates my back teeth. "We got her where we wants her. Oh, Prinny, you'll wish you never opened your mouth on that bus."

Prinny's poised at the very end of the wharf where the foghorn stands on its tall metal posts. Not a truck in sight. All the men must have gone home before we got here.

What's she gonna do? Jump in?

She can't do that. It's early June, the water bone-cracking cold.

The foghorn blasts. Because we're standing plumb underneath it, I nearly jump out of my jacket. Mel surges toward Prinny, who drops her backpack near the creosoted boards and before you know it she's over the top and down the metal ladder. I run to the edge of the wharf. Prinny's on the bottom rung, untying the hawser on her father's wooden dory. She jumps in, gripping the gunwales for balance as the dory dips and sways.

Tate shrieks a cussword, throwing herself down the ladder. Mel picks up a rock and fires it at Prinny. But Prinny's already grabbed the oars, using one of them to push off from the wharf, and the rock plops into the slow, black heave of the sea. She plunks down on the thwart and takes a hard stroke with the other oar. The bow turns away from the pilings.

Tate lunges for the stern.

Prinny takes another stroke, both oars this time, putting her back into it, rowing as if her life depends on it. Mel snags an old gaff off the wharf, takes aim, and tosses it like it's an Olympic javelin. The rusty prongs scrape Prinny's arm, the long wooden handle tangling with an oar. The dory yaws.

The gaff slides into the sea and floats away, bobbing on the waves. As Prinny digs in the oars again, Mel flings a rock that grazes Prinny's cheek.

Then the dory's swallowed by the fog, leaving small, flat circles on the swell where the oars dipped in. Tate's still clinging to the bottom of the ladder. A wave sloshes over her sneakers but I'm not sure she even feels it. Savage, that's how she looks. Like she could throttle Prinny with her bare hands.

I notice something else. The tide's turned. From high to low.

A lump of ice lodges itself in my chest.

Seal, my stepdad, taught me about the tides in the cove; when the tide's going out, the current can pull you past the rocks at the entrance to the cove and out to sea. Out to the offshore reef we call Knucklebones that can tear open the boards of a dory like it's made of paper.

I sidle backwards, quiet-like so Mel won't notice. For the first time that afternoon, I'm glad of the fog. I slide into it, and as soon as Mel blurs into nothing, I whirl like Prinny and run fast as I can. Past ropes and barrels, past the old fish shack where Danny Grimsby used to store his gear and no one with the heart to pull it down, until I come to the big building with its Government of Canada sign and its list of regulations longer than any list at school. Fingers shaking, I pull out my smartphone.

It's shut down. Battery's zapped.

Home. I gotta go home.

Up the slope, dodging the potholes. Thud of my steps. Clap of my heartbeat. Daren't stop to listen for Tate and Mel.

What'll I do if Seal's home?

Keeping to the shoulder of the road, I pound past Cole's house, then Buck's with its pretty pink petunias in wooden pots at the end of his driveway. Scruffy spruce trees and a tangle of alders between me and the sea.

Our bungalow looms out of the fog. No vehicles in the driveway. With a sob of relief I run up the path and unlock the front door. Through the living room into the kitchen, take out the phone book and flip through the pages for St. Fabien because Ratchet, where Prinny lives, is too small to have its own section.

Murphy, a whole row of Murphys, and there's Thomas Murphy. I block Call Display and punch in the numbers. One ring, two, then a man says, "Yeah?"

Prinny's father. Gasping for air, I say in a high-pitched voice I hope sounds like a little kid's, "You gotta go to the wharf. Prinny's in a dory rowing out to sea and the tide's turned. Go rescue her—hurry!" Then I slam the phone down.

Tate and Mel will be wondering where I am.

Out the door, down the path and back the way I came, fear nipping at my heels.

What am I more afraid of? Prinny drowning on the reef? Or Tate and Mel?

Two

to deceive

My sneakers rasp in the gravel at the edge of the road. I should try out for Track and Field next year. Only three weeks left of being in grade six.

Prinny, stay in the cove, don't get pulled out to Knucklebones...

Down the slope, past the government building, everything in reverse. I slow down, trying to control my breathing. *Act cool, Sigrid.* You had to go home and use the washroom, that'll be your excuse.

All of a sudden—too sudden—Tate's right in front of me. "Where you been?"

"I—I had to run home. Must've been the hamburger I reheated for supper last night. Thought it tasted off at the time but I was hungry and—"

"Who's at your place?"

"No one. But Seal could be home anytime. I told you it's his day off."

"Poor little Sigrid, aren't you allowed to invite your friends in?"

"Yes! But—"

"My feet are wet. You can loan me dry socks. And Prinny will hang out in the cove for a while...we'll check back in half an hour."

"Yeah," Mel says, "we'll fix Prinny's clock once we've warmed up."

Does she have to make it so obvious she's looking forward to it?

We climb the slope, Tate, then Mel, then me. Did I leave the phone book open on the table, or did I shove it back in the drawer? I can't remember, dread so heavy on my shoulders I stumble into a pothole and have to grab Mel's windbreaker for support.

She gives me a nasty look over her shoulder. "Quit it."

"Sorry."

Seal's not home. They walk in my front door and into the living room. Mel leaves her sneakers on. Tate kicks hers off and slops across the floor in her wet socks. I know the place is a mess, but still.

I say brightly, "Make yourselves at home. I'll bring in some chips."

I hear the creak of springs as Mel settles on the couch. In the kitchen, the phone book is open on the table. I jam it back into the drawer just as Tate stations herself in the doorway. "Dry socks," she says, snappy-like.

"Sorry. Forgot."

I find an old brown pair in my drawer and pass them to her. She peels off the wet ones, dropping them on my bedroom floor. Then she follows me back to the kitchen, and watches as I take a bag of chips out of the cupboard.

"Sour cream and onion?" she says. "My least favorite."

"It's all there is. Seal does groceries tomorrow."

My mother isn't into buying groceries. Or doing anything else that smacks of the kind of housework normal mothers do.

"No nachos?" Tate says, right snarky.

The TV's blaring in the living room; Mel likes the kids' channels.

"You want to check the pantry?" I say. "I'll pour some pop."

Tate marches into the pantry, shoving stuff around with maximum noise. I take a bottle of Pepsi out of the fridge. It's not that far from Ratchet to Fiddlers Cove, and Prinny's father knows how treacherous the waters off the cove can be. He'll hurry. I know he will.

Tate snaps, "Not a single thing that's edible in here."

"Crackers," I say. "There's some Cheez Whiz in the fridge. Open the crackers, Tate, and I'll whip us up a snack."

So that's what I do, chattering away about the new spandex jeans I bought last weekend. Tate watches me, drumming her fingers on the counter. Only time you see Tate relaxed is when some poor sucker's just handed over her life's savings. Or his life's savings. Either way is fine with her.

Mel's surfing with the remote to dodge the commercials. I pass Tate the crackers. Mel chows down on the chips. Last thing she should be eating, given her weight.

What if Prinny's already been swept out to sea?

I spring up from the couch and march into Lorne's room. Lorne's my big brother and *messy* is his middle name. In the clutter on his bureau are two unopened bags of nachos.

"Here, Tate," I say, passing them to her.

"Great!" She glances up and smiles at me, a real smile, like a 100-watt bulb came on. I wish she'd do that more often.

The minutes creep by. Tate checks her watch, paid for by Prinny, Vi, and Avery. "We'll leave Prinny for another day. I better go home."

Tate lives two doors up from me. Her parents belong to The Congregation of the Sacred Brotherhood. Her mother works at the religious bookstore in town. Her father sells life insurance, which seems strange for a guy who, according to gossip, talks to God on an hourly basis. His eyes make me think of icebergs, that cold, pale blue.

Mel says, "So I gotta hoof it home? Or hitch?"

"Guess so," Tate says.

Standing by the window, I watch them walk down the

path. As Tate heads east and Mel west, they vanish into the fog.

Please, Prinny, be safe....

THREE

to fret

Seal and Lorne don't come home for supper, although at least Seal calls to tell me; my mother doesn't turn up, big surprise. Even though I'm not hungry—my gut's in a knot—I microwave a small double-cheese pizza, and chew on it, gazing through the living-room window at the road.

Old Danny Grimsby limps past; he was a fisherman, who took to the booze after his only son drowned off Knucklebones years ago. Right now, he's in no rush, not like he would be if Prinny was lost at sea.

A few minutes later, Hud Quinn bikes down the road, his knees sticking out because he needs a bigger bicycle. He's in grade eight, and he's Tate's rival for bully-in-chief along our section of the shore, although he never bullies girls. His favorite target is Travis Keating.

Hud isn't in a hurry, either.

At six-thirty, my brother Lorne's souped-up Honda roars into our driveway. Lorne slams the car door, slams the front door, and grins at me. "Hey."

"Anything new?" I say, real casual.

"In this dump?" he says cheerfully. "Nah...d'you need the bathroom?"

Hope spears my chest. Seems like Prinny might, just might, be okay. If she was stuck on one of the reefs, Danny, Hud, and Lorne would know about it. Only one thing travels faster than a nor'easter along our shore, and that's gossip.

"Bathroom, Sigrid?" Lorne repeats. "Do you need it? Big date."

"All your dates are big."

"Girls go for me," he says. "I should complain?"

Lorne's nineteen, tall, with broad shoulders because he works out at the gym, and—you know that phrase, *happy-go-lucky?* That's Lorne. Hardly ever buys a lottery ticket but he wins something. Lands a job as a mechanic at the garage in St. Fabien first time he applies. Smiles at a pretty girl and she smiles back.

"So who is it tonight?" I say.

"Sally Parsons. It's been her for the last three weeks."

I roll my eyes. "A new record. Don't leave your wet towels all over the floor." He gives my hair a playful tug, shucks his jacket onto the couch, and kicks off his work boots where they're guaranteed to trip the next person who comes along. His bedroom door slams.

Twenty minutes later he leaves, whistling, his hair in damp curls for Sally Parsons to run her fingers through.

I stand at the window, watching him drive away. I wish

I could phone someone like Travis, or Laice Hadden, and find out for sure that Prinny's okay. But Travis and Laice don't like me because I'm a Shrike.

With a sigh, I turn around. Dust bunnies are gathered in little flocks on the living-room floor. I could sweep. Or I could wash the dishes. I don't feel like doing either one.

Back when my friend Hanna still lived in Fiddlers Cove, on a Friday night with summer just around the corner we'd have been together, at my place or hers. We'd have the radio on—disco, bluegrass, heavy metal, country, didn't matter—and we'd be dancing up a storm, just the two of us.

Her mother, who was real nice, taught us how to move to *Flashdance,* how to jive and do the hip-hop.

I gave up dancing when Hanna left.

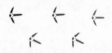

Seal arrives home at nine-thirty. He doesn't tell me where he's been all day. Ruffling my hair, his blue eyes smiling, he says, "I have tomorrow off, too, because of those extra shifts last week. Think the liquor store can manage without me for two days?"

My own smile feels stiff. "Any news worth hearing?"

"Same old, same old."

I swear every muscle in my body goes slack, I'm that

relieved. "What are you up to tomorrow?"

"Meeting my buddies at Tim Hortons." Where, like usual, they'll ignore the twenty-minute rule and stretch their double-doubles over a good two hours.

"We need to do groceries."

"You make the list and I'll call you before I leave Tim's."

Tim Hortons, FoodMart, the mall, and the liquor store are all in St. Fabien, the only town of any size in our area.

I give Seal a hug, go to bed, and sleep okay because Prinny's safe.

At quarter to nine the next morning, someone knocks on the front door.

It's a solid front door, not the kind with glass so you can peek at who's there. I open it. Prinny Murphy is standing on the path, holding her bike. My knees go so weak that I sag against the door frame.

She says, "Thank you for phoning my place last night."

She doesn't sound friendly and she doesn't sound grateful.

"How'd you know it was me?"

"Mel doesn't have the smarts to know I was in trouble, and Tate wouldn't care if I ended up on the rocks. Had to be you."

"Oh."

"Besides, you know about boats and the tides."

My tongue fumbles with the words. "Did you make it back on your own?"

"Da came out in his speedboat, towed me back to the wharf."

"You gonna tell Tate I called?"

Her eyes are as cool as rainwater. "No."

The weight of every rock in Newfoundland slides off my shoulders. "Thanks."

"I was being washed out of the cove when Da found me. He doesn't get mad often, but when he does, watch out."

I've seen Prinny's father lots of times. Slow-moving in his overalls and white t-shirt, with an easy smile. *A good man to haul traps with,* according to the fishermen, who aren't known for doling out praise.

"What do you mean?" I say. "What will he do?"

Neatly, Prinny turns her bike around and marches down the path to the road, her shiny ponytail swinging from side to side. I take two steps after her, then stop. She didn't answer on purpose. Wants me to suffer.

I think of her rowing through the fog, the black swell, the growl of waves breaking on the rocks...

She rides away, not a backward look. Dandelions sprouting all over our lawn like the happy faces you can insert in your emails if you're in a happy-face mood.

I go back inside. Every now and then I've imagined Prinny knocking on my front door and asking me if I'd like to be her friend.

Like that'll happen.

Will her father come after me? Will he tell Seal and my mother? Seal doesn't know I'm a Shrike, one of three bullies who specialize in extortion. It's not something you advertise.

He'd be horrified. Worse than horrified. Lorne wouldn't think much of it, either.

I go into my room and sit on my bed, hunched over, my nerves in an uproar. I wait for them to settle. I wait for Prinny's father to pound on the front door or the cops to come and arrest me. When the phone shrills, I jump halfway to the ceiling.

Very slowly I walk to the kitchen, counting the rings.

Call Display shows Seal's cell. I snatch up the receiver before it goes to voice mail.

"I'm ready to leave Tim Hortons," he says. "I just talked to your mother. She's gone for the weekend, back on Monday morning."

What do you want me to say? That I'll miss her?

He sighs. "Have you made a grocery list?"

"By the time you get here, I'll have it ready."

Quickly, I check the cupboards and the fridge, pencil

in hand. Hard to make a list when you never know who'll be home. Harder still when every little sound sets your nerves flapping in your gut like trapped ravens.

When Seal pulls into the driveway, I run outdoors. He leans over and unlatches the passenger door, pushing it partway open. He's nice that way. Treats me like I deserve his good manners and his friendly smile. There's times I wonder if he's trying to make up for my mother, but mostly I don't believe that. He's just a decent guy, with rusty-red hair and the bluest eyes of anyone the length of the shore. I smile back, and for a minute the thought of Prinny's angry father doesn't seem so desperate.

FoodMart is busy, so it takes us a while to go through the list. Then we head home. As we're lugging the bags in, he says, awkward for him, "Guess I won't be home for supper, Sigrid. You be okay?"

"Sure." He's busy lifting a big box of corn flakes out of the bag. "You weren't home last night, either."

He vanishes into the pantry. "I should be home tomorrow."

Should be isn't the same as *will be.* "You playing poker tonight?"

He stashes pizza in the freezer compartment. "Not tonight."

So don't tell me what you're up to. See if I care.

Some days it's like everyone's got a life but me. And don't I hate it when I whine.

Four

to summon

The weekend crawls by. Not a sign of Prinny's father. Most people, when they're angry, act on it right away. So you'd think I'd relax as hour by hour passes and nothing happens.

You'd think wrong.

I bicycle to Gulley Cove on Sunday for something to do and because I know I won't run into Tate—she's never allowed out on Sundays. Too busy being part of the Brotherhood. The one time I asked her where the Sisterhood was located, she nearly crawled down my throat.

There used to be a bunch of feral cats at Gulley Cove until Travis rescued them. He found homes for most of them, although one or two still live in Abe Murphy's barn just up the road. Travis is another decent guy, and cute besides.

I have the cove to myself. I'm not much for the outdoors, but it's peaceful here, waves wallowing on the rocks, the boards of the staging warm in the sun. I almost forget that I'm a Shrike who's all stressed out about Prinny's da.

The day I first heard that name, Shrike, I Googled it. Guess what? A shrike is a bird that shoves its prey, which you truly hope is dead, onto a sharp thorn and leaves it there until dinnertime. Sort of like our pantry. Isn't that enough to put anyone off the great outdoors?

Seal doesn't come home for supper. Lorne does. Sally's working, he says, and parks himself in front of our old TV with a plate of spaghetti on his lap. Although he slurps up the long, slippery strands with maximum noise, for once that doesn't irritate me. I'm just glad of the company.

Funny thing about Lorne—he doesn't get riled up about our mother, not like I do. And him and Seal were best buddies from the get-go.

Finally it's time for bed.

I lie flat on my back in the dark, listening to the mutter of voices from whatever show he's watching. Nothing's going to happen tomorrow. Prinny is safe, her father's over his mad, and if Prinny said she won't rat on me to Tate, she won't.

Quit being a wuss, that's what I tell myself.

While Tate and me are waiting for the school bus, Cole and Buck bat a beat-up tennis ball back and forth with their hockey sticks. Tate inserts her earrings—ugly metal chains—and loops more chains from her belt. Then she slicks red lip gloss on her mouth and piles mascara on her lashes. One day when she was in a good mood, she told me that all of them are against the rules of the Brotherhood.

She's not even allowed to own a bicycle. She rides tandem with Mel.

Admiring her reflection in her little mirror, she says, "My cousin Melissa, the one who lives in Ratchet, saw Prinny on the weekend—none the worse for her little boat trip. We'll up the pressure on her today. At recess."

"We should lay off Prinny Murphy!"

"When I wants your opinion, I'll ask for it."

"You're the brains of our little group, Tate. We're just lucky Prinny didn't end up on the rocks."

"Back off or I'll sic Mel on you!"

"Here comes the bus," I say.

Mel can't touch me on the bus because Mr. Murphy, our driver—he's another of the Murphys from Ratchet—is death on bullying. He might have gray hair, but he could pick up any kid on the bus in one hand and every kid on the bus knows it. Even Hud, who rarely misses a chance to bully Travis, never kicks or punches him on the bus.

At school, I run for the main door. The other kids give me a wide berth, like usual.

Tate and Mel disappear into the girls' washroom to collect Vi's twenty dollars. I go straight to my desk in our homeroom. I'm safe here. Mrs. Dooks, our teacher, is a pro at keeping everyone in line.

Safe doesn't last very long.

At 9:30 an announcement comes over the loudspeaker from the school secretary, her voice crackling into the room. "Prinny Murphy, Tate Cody, Mel Corkum, and Sigrid Sugden: please come to the principal's office immediately. Thank you."

I sit there, frozen as a High Liner cod fillet. Prinny's father. He held onto his mad until this morning.

When Tate finds out I phoned him, she'll kill me.

With the all-too-willing help of Mel.

Mrs. Dooks says, "Hurry up, Sigrid! All of you, right back to class afterwards. We'll be reviewing for exams."

I stumble to my feet. Prinny's already halfway down the corridor, Tate hot on her heels, Mel thumping along behind them. I'm the last one to walk past the secretary with her crystal earrings and fuzzy mauve sweater.

In the principal's office, Prinny's father is standing with his back to the wall so he can see who comes through the door. Mr. MacInney, bald as a plucked chicken, is seated behind his desk. His eyes look like they've seen everything there is to see and he could do without most of it.

We all sit down. Black metal chair, cold through my jeans. I wrap my fingers around the edges, hold on tight like I'm the one in a dory with the tide on the turn.

Mr. MacInney says, "It has come to my attention that you three girls are responsible for what all too easily could have been a tragedy. On Friday afternoon, Prinny went to the wharf in Fiddlers Cove to speak to her father. Unfortunately, he had already left for home. He's here today to lay a complaint that you terrorized his daughter that afternoon. Although she managed to escape in a dory, she was nearly swept out to sea. What do you have to say for yourselves?"

Silence thicker than fog. Then Tate says, "If Prinny was stupid enough to go rowing in the cove, that's her problem."

"Do you admit you were on the wharf in Fiddlers Cove on Friday afternoon?"

"I don't admit nuthin'."

"Anything," he says. "Mel?"

Mel frowns at Tate. "We was on the wharf Friday. Last day of the week—that's how come I remember."

Tate shoots her a vicious look.

"So you *were* on the wharf, Tate," Mr. MacInney says, making a note on his pad.

"Is that a crime?"

"Failure to admit the truth," he says, writing away. "Were you bullying Prinny?"

"We was minding our own business." She sneers at him. "Anyways, what's the big deal—she's sitting right here in this room, ain't she?"

Mr. MacInney skewers her with the stare that shows why he's been voted Principal of the Year for five years in a row. "Luckily for all concerned, Prinny's father went back to the wharf. He had to go out in his speedboat to rescue his daughter. This is a very serious matter, Tate."

Her eyes drop first. Mr. MacInney turns the stare on me. "Sigrid? What about you?"

My brain's in a scramble. Didn't Prinny's da tell him about the phone call? "I got nothing to say."

"I've heard rumors about you three, "Mr. MacInney says, "but no one's ever been willing to give me concrete details. So I've had to ignore the rumors for lack of evidence. Prinny wouldn't under any circumstances other than extreme threat have left the wharf in a dory in thick fog with the tide going out—she's too experienced on the water. I want to know which of you was the ringleader."

"Ringleader?" Mel says with a baffled frown, spreading her fingers as though they're circled with gold.

"Whose idea was it to chase Prinny into the dory?"

"She's the one climbed in the dory. It was her idea," Mel says triumphantly.

"Shut up," Tate says.

"I see," Mr. MacInney says. "Sigrid? Do you have anything to add?"

I shake my head.

"Very well. Prinny's father has asked to meet with your parents in my office this evening, and I've placed the calls. The secretary will escort you back to class, and you're to stay inside at recess and lunch hour, where you'll be supervised at all times."

Prinny's da hasn't said one word. But the way he's standing against the wall—no little metal chair for him—solid as the wharf, that's how he looks, and just as unmoveable. We file out and march in a straight line down the corridor, the secretary's high heels rapping on the tiles.

Mr. MacInney and Prinny's da—they're saving the phone call for tonight. I feel like I might throw up.

Back in class, Mrs. Dooks says, "Page 126. Open your book, Sigrid. What are the two main metaphors in the poem?"

The words jiggle on the page. "Um. The rising sun as hope?"

"And the second one?" she says impatiently.

"The mist over the lake. Despair."

Maybe there's a point to poetry after all.

We're supervised at recess by Mr. Marsden, who's obviously been told to keep his eye on us, and at lunch hour by Mrs. Dooks, who's not too happy to have an added chore foisted on her. When it's time to catch the bus, I dawdle through the thinning crowd of kids, and sneak to the bus from the back end, hoping Tate and Mel are already on board.

DO NOT PASS WHEN RED LIGHTS FLASHING.

I edge around the back fender. Tate's flattened against the rear wheel, where Mr. Murphy can't see her. My heart slaps my ribs. I turn to run, but Mel comes from nowhere—she can move real fast when she's got a kid in her sights. Her fingers circle my arm, nearly hoisting me off my feet.

Tate smiles. Mel yanks my arm behind my back and pulls up. Simplest move in the book. Most painful for the effort it takes. I haven't been a Shrike for nothing.

I can't help it, I whimper.

"Ringleader," Tate says. "We all know Mel's not ringleader material. So that leaves you and me, Sigrid. Tonight you'll tell 'em it was your idea to chase Prinny into the dory."

Right. I chase Prinny into the dory then I call her father to come and rescue her out of the dory.

Tate says, her eyes narrowing, "Another little tug there, Mel."

Mel tugs. I yelp.

"I guess that means *yes*," Tate says. She shoves her face at mine. "I've had time to come up with a few questions. On Friday, why did you run home? Rotten hamburger, Sigrid? Or did you warn Prinny's father that she was out in the dory? And that's why he went back to the wharf?"

"He must've forgotten something—that's why he went back. The hamburger *was* rotten."

Tate nods at Mel. Mel tugs. Tears spring to my eyes, and Tate smiles again. "Enough for now, Mel—we're holding up the bus. But if you ratted on us, Sigrid, this is just a taste of what's to come."

Mel lets go. I breathe shallow-like and follow them onto the bus.

To my huge relief, Mel gets off in Long Bight. Tate, Buck, Cole, and me get off at the first stop in Fiddlers Cove. Cole and Buck hit the ground on the run, bashing their hockey sticks on the road, and disappear up Cole's driveway. Tate does her chain-routine in reverse, slipping them into her backpack, then scrubbing off her lipstick and dropping the Kleenex on the ground. "See you this evening," she says.

Mel is two miles west of us, and what have I got to lose? "Prinny's father goes back and forth to the wharf all the time. Don't you get it, Tate? If he hadn't shown up, Prinny could've drowned."

Tate shrugs. "If she did, no one would've been any the wiser."

My jaw drops. "What d'you mean?"

"Who knew we were at the wharf? No witnesses."

"Did you *want* her to drown?"

"I wouldn't have cared one way or the other."

"I don't believe you!"

"That's your problem," she says, and saunters away.

She was joking. Of course she was.

If she wasn't...if she really didn't care...is that where I'm headed if I keep on being a Shrike?

I run for the house, lock the front door and the sliding-glass doors off the kitchen-slash-dining room, and stare out at the barrens. Rock, scrub, and bog for miles and no place to hide.

FIVE

to accuse

My mother drives into the yard in her flashy Chevy Camaro at six on the nose, and flounces into the house in a rhinestone-studded sweater, an embroidered denim vest, and jeans decorated with swirls of black beads. Fake-alligator boots on her feet.

"You still live here?" I say.

"Don't you sass me!"

Let's get this over with. My mother, Lissie Sugden, and her friend Ady Melanson are eBay sellers. Big time. At Ady's place, they glue themselves to the computer to keep track of prices. They do the rounds of thrift shops, yard sales, and auctions, their noses keener for bargains than a bloodhound's for clues. And since the spring, they've started going on buying trips to Corner Brook and Grand Falls, staying away two and three days at a time. The thrill of the chase—that's what my mother loves.

I never call her *Mom. Mom* is for apple-pie mothers, for white-shirts-pegged-to-the-clothesline mothers. If I call her anything, it's *Ma.*

She sits down at the table. She's pretty, did I say

that? Very pretty.

Supper is KD and a salad from FoodMart that Seal brought home. The three of us eating together...how often does that happen?

Jabbing her fork at me, she says, "What's this all about? Dragging me away from a sale on linens and bathware."

"You'll find out."

"Why wouldn't the principal tell me what's going on? Did he tell you, Seal?"

"No."

Her knife clatters against the side of her plate. "How long will it take?"

"I dunno," I say.

"What *is* going on, Sigrid?" Seal says.

His voice is level, but I can tell he's upset. "Your marks are good," he says, "and your attendance. Has something happened on the bus? Are kids picking on you?"

"No," I say, "no one's picking on me."

"Were you rude to your teacher? Mrs. Dooks can be tough, but only because she wants you to learn."

"No."

"You haven't been skipping classes?"

"Not really."

"Either you have or you haven't," he says, sharp for him.

"I skipped Friday—quit bugging me, Seal! You'll find out soon enough."

"It had better be for a good reason, that's all I can say," my mother announces, tossing her blonde curls like she's a teenager on her way to the prom.

She pushes her plate aside and disappears into their bedroom to change her clothes, leaving me and Seal to put away the leftovers. As I reach for a plastic container, the tension is as thick as the KD.

My mother decides that a very short dress and stiletto heels are appropriate attire when your daughter's being hauled in front of the principal. Seal changes his shirt.

She takes the Camaro. Seal and I follow in the truck.

We're the second ones to arrive, at two minutes to seven. Prinny's mom looks right pretty now she's laid off the booze, although it's a different kind of prettiness from my mother's. My mother has *don't touch* written all over her. Prinny's mom—she'd be nice to hug. She's clinging to her husband's arm, him towering over her in his overalls and a white t-shirt.

Mr. MacInney is doodling on his notepad. He looks up when we walk in. "Let's get started."

"But the rest aren't here," I blurt.

"They're coming later."

I gape at him. What's going on?

He goes through his spiel, detailing the rumors he's heard about me, Tate, and Mel, then briefly describing the events of Friday afternoon. He finishes by saying, "Although none of them will admit it, I believe Tate is the ringleader of the group."

Seal says slowly, "Have I got this right, Sigrid? You and these other two girls have been bullying kids? Not just last Friday. All along."

He sounds so disbelieving that I want to sink through the tiled floor.

My mother says, "There was a show on TV about the children of divorce. Because they're unhappy, they pick on other kids. Sigrid's father abandoned her. It's his fault."

I'm not sure Seal hears one word of this. He's still staring at me, as though I've sprouted bright red horns.

Mr. MacInney says, "Luckily Sigrid had the good sense to phone Prinny's parents right away on Friday and warn them that their daughter was in danger. Which, of course, is why I know Sigrid wasn't the ringleader."

Prinny's father squints at me. "I thank you, Sigrid, for at least making that phone call. Likely you need to sit down and think things through. Decide if you're gonna be part of the problem or part of the solution."

Mr. MacInney waits for me to say something. I stare at the floor. The silence stretches out until Prinny's da says, "I'm not laying charges, even though there's plenty of evidence. But one more whiff of trouble from you, Sigrid, and I'll put the cops onto you."

Seal's breath hisses between his teeth.

The principal folds his hands on his desk. "I think that's all we need to say for now. I'm having two more meetings this evening—one with Tate's parents and one with Mel's father. There's no need for them to know about the phone call." He gives me his *I've-seen-it-all* look. "Although you've gotten in with some bad company, Sigrid, you're being given the chance to change that situation. I strongly suggest you end your association with Tate and Mel."

"Yes, sir," I say. And how am I supposed to do that?

Seal says, "Thank you, Mr. MacInney. We'll be watching Sigrid very closely from now on."

The three of us leave the office. When we're outside, my mother says, "I'm going to Ady's. A feather bed with a three-year guarantee is scheduled for this evening."

Seal looks like a mackerel hook is stuck in his arm and someone's yanking on it. "You should stay home for once!"

"Like I said, everything's Randy's fault. He's the one who left us in the lurch by going out west and never coming back. Divorce is extremely high on the stress list—it's been scientifically proved."

"You're just like Randy, Lissie, except you take off to Ady's and leave the rest of us in the lurch."

"Don't be so foolish," she says, gets in her car, flicks on her signal lights, and turns up the street toward Ady's.

Seal jams his seat belt into the slot. Then he surges out of the schoolyard.

I have the sense to keep my mouth shut.

Six

to hack

After we get home, Seal says, "Sit down a minute. I need to get to the bottom of this. *Are* you unhappy because of your dad?"

I'm way beyond unhappy and it's nothing to do with Randy Sugden. Terror is what's churning in my gut, terror weighted with despair because I don't see how I'll ever be free of this mess. "I won't be hanging with Tate and Mel anymore," I say.

"Do you still miss your real dad?"

"He's been gone since I was five."

"I asked you a question!"

Seal almost never gets riled and this is twice in one evening. "I dunno," I say sulkily.

"I thought you were a good kid. And now I find out you've been bullying other kids—and not just once or twice. You disappoint me, Sigrid."

It's like he's hauled my arm behind my back and he's tugging on it. "Tate's the planner and Mel's the one who does the heavy-duty stuff!"

"And where are you? Standing around watching?"

"Well, not exactly. But—"

"I don't want to see you near Tate and Mel ever again. And I want you to make some new friends."

I pick at the seam of my jeans.

Seal has lots of friends, for all that he's not from here. He was born on Fogo Island, where he used to fish, and I know he misses his old home and his boat. His problem is, he fell in love with my mother. Her blonde curls and big brown eyes, the way she has of looking helpless.

When I was seven and eight, he took the trouble to teach me how to row, how to read the tides in the cove and watch the sky for changes in the weather. I should tell him that he's always been a good stepdad, better than good, but the words catch in my throat.

He says, talking slow, like he's searching out the words. "I guess I don't understand...I never thought you had a mean bone in you, and now I find out you scared Prinny Murphy so bad she rowed a dory into the fog. Seems I haven't been paying enough attention." He sits down heavily on the arm of the couch, his shoulders rounded as if ten Sigrids are perched on them. "You know what this means? I'll have to keep a close watch on you from now on. Like you're seven years old, not twelve."

I was seven when he moved in with my mother and he sure knows how to twist the knife. "Sorry," I mutter.

"I work full-time and we can't count on your mother.

So I'll be trusting you to behave when I'm not home. Can I trust you?"

I nod, rubbing an old stain on the cushion with one finger. "Are you gonna tell Lorne?"

"Wasn't planning on it."

"Please don't!"

He gives a heavy sigh. "You load the dishwasher, and I'll clean up the pots."

I stick a couple of plates in the bottom rack. So he thinks I should quit seeing Tate and Mel and make some new friends.

When Hanna moved away two years ago, I decided right then and there that I'd never have another best friend. Not long after, Tate started inviting me places, and I opted for *mean* instead, for pushing my anger into everyone else's face because if I was hurting so bad, why shouldn't they?

Six months of being mean was more than enough. But by then I was in too deep, and way too scared of Tate and Mel, to be able to quit being a Shrike.

Seal never noticed that I'd changed from *nice* to *mean.* Even though I did my best to make sure he didn't notice, I'm still mad at him for not noticing.

When I get up the next morning, the Camaro's already

gone from the driveway. I take my time in the shower, in the hopes that hot water will loosen the tightness between my shoulders. After wrapping my wet hair in a towel, I get dressed, and wipe the steam off the mirror.

I'm not pretty like my mother. I'm ordinary. Tidy-like, all my features in the right place. Brown hair, brown eyebrows, brown eyes. Straight nose, mouth that's not too big and not too small, teeth in even rows. You'd never pick me out from those line-ups they have in police stations when they want to nail the suspect.

Mind you, a bit of make-up—mascara and eye shadow, blusher—can do wonders. I have to go easy, though. Seal's none too keen on not-yet-thirteen-year-olds wearing mascara.

I watch through the living-room window until I see the bus coming down the road from Ratchet before I go outdoors. Tate's already there.

Something about her is different.

When I walk closer, I see what it is. Her hair, her long, shiny black hair, has been chopped off in short, jagged clumps that stick out every which way. Like a prison haircut. Like the person who did it hated her.

She's not wearing her chain earrings or her lipstick.

She says in a brittle voice, "If you say one word, I'll rip you to shreds."

I want to say *I'm sorry,* and how bizarre is that?

The bus stops beside us. I climb on last, after Tate,

Cole, and Buck. Even Mr. Murphy looks shocked when he sees the ruination of Tate's hair.

Every kid on the bus is staring at her: Travis, who rescues anyone or anything that needs rescuing; Prinny, who has plenty of reasons to hate the Shrikes; Hector Baldwin, whose ears stick out and who hardly ever opens his gob; snooty Laice Hadden, from the big city of Halifax; the Herbey girls, Taylor and Brianna, who never have a sensible word to say between them; and last of all, Hud, with his gray eyes that reveal absolutely nothing.

I sit across from Tate. She ignores me. A few minutes later, we pick up Mel and the rest of the Long Bight kids. Mel looks awful, hair in greasy strands, eyes still red like she spent the night crying.

Tate clears her throat. Then she says, loud enough for the whole bus to hear, "Sigrid, did you know your stepdad's dating Davina Murphy?"

Stepdad...dating? What's she talking about?

"Guess that's news to you," she says. "Davina lives in Ratchet. Her husband died three years ago."

I've seen Davina Murphy at Baldwin's store in Ratchet. She's like me, ordinary. Not pretty or glamorous like my mother. I clamp my jaws shut so I won't ask any of the questions twanging in my brain.

Tate sneers at me. "My cousin Melissa told me Seal's truck has been parked outside Davina's place lots of evenings the last while."

A hard lump settles in my belly. Seal wouldn't tell me where he was going Saturday night. He didn't show up for Sunday dinner even though he'd said he likely would. And the reason he's been keeping it a secret is because he's still living with my mother even though she's hardly ever home to be lived with.

If Seal moves out on me...that only leaves Lorne.

From kindergarten up, I've never been the most popular girl in school, nowhere close. But today it seems like everyone takes extra big steps around me. Text messages flying, girls giggling, guys eyeing me like I'm some kind of monster.

I ignore them all, my face like those guys Lorne watches playing poker on TV.

As we leave the classroom for recess, Travis says to me, and he's kind enough to keep his voice low, "Prinny could've drowned last Friday. Yeah, you made the phone call. But you also helped scare her into the dory. Bad move, Sigrid."

He's as tall as me now because he grew a lot this spring. I blink back tears, wondering why he can hurt me when a gaggle of girls can't.

I don't take any chances at recess. I park myself against the wall near Mr. Marsden and I don't budge. Tate and

Mel watch me for the entire fifteen minutes, Tate's ugly hanks of hair lifting in the wind, Mel fidgeting because she can't wait to get her hands on me.

No one, but no one, says anything to Tate about the new haircut.

Lunchtime in the cafeteria, I sit at the table beside the cashier. I'm doing okay. After school, all I have to do is run for the house and lock the doors.

Mel doesn't get off in Long Bight. I chew the inside of my lip until it bleeds. When the bus pulls up at my stop in Fiddlers Cove, I whisper to Mr. Murphy, "Would you wait until I'm in the house before you drive away? Please?"

"Sure," he says, and smiles at me.

I stumble down the steps, run up the path and in the front door. Lock it, race for the glass doors in the kitchen, bang the white plastic latch down, and fit the shaft of Lorne's old hockey stick into the groove so no one can open the door. Then I look up.

Tate and Mel are standing outside, Mel's pug nose squashed against the glass, her face a hideous mask. Tate smiles. Teeth only. I rattle the curtains across their metal rod, then run from room to room, checking that every window in the place is closed.

A few minutes later, the phone rings. Tate's cell. I don't pick up.

Her voice leaps into the room because the phone's on Speaker. "I've remembered something, Sigrid—last

Friday, I noticed you shoving the phone book back in the drawer when I walked in the kitchen in my wet socks. Didn't realize it meant anything at the time. So you *did* phone Prinny's dad...that's why Mr. MacInney had separate meetings with our parents. Because he didn't want the rest of us to know. And that's how he figured out I was the ringleader."

When she laughs, my heart almost stops beating. "You'd have been better off letting us in today. The longer we has to wait, the worse it'll be."

The phone clicks off. I'm shivering.

It's 4:10. I can't go out on my bike. I can't sit on the patio. I don't want to do my homework. I hardly ever watch TV, in case the Shopping Channel turns me into a bargain-hunting maniac.

Mrs. Dooks told us about some activist in Burma who was under house arrest for years and years. At the time, I thought, *no big deal.*

SEVEN

to defend

It's sunny and warm the next day. I repeat my safety measures at recess and in the cafeteria. I only go to the washroom when I know it'll be crowded.

Mel stays on the bus all the way to Fiddlers Cove for the second day in a row. Mr. Murphy waits until I'm in the front door. I lock it and hurry to the sliding doors, which Lorne or Seal must've left open. The plastic catch won't go down. I push on it, sweating, and hear a noise that makes my hair stand on end.

The window in Lorne's room. Rasp of the screen. Scraping sounds like someone's climbing over the sill. Has to be Tate, she's the small one, the agile one. As I run from the kitchen through the living room, I hear twin thumps as she lands on the floor. Jerking the latch sideways, I'm out the front door.

Mel is standing square in the path.

I dart across the lawn, but she moves fast, grabbing the hem of my t-shirt. Twisting, I try to tug free. She sticks out a foot and down I go. I curl into myself and roll, but before I can stand up, she's kicking me.

Levering myself on one elbow, I claw at her knee just as Tate rushes up. She hauls on my arm, yanks me around, and slaps me across the nose. The dandelions smear into yellow streaks as I hit the ground.

"That's just a start," she says. "Me and Mel aren't allowed to get together anymore—and it's all your fault. You and your big mouth!"

Mel pulls me to my feet, shaking me like I'm a puppy. My neck flops. My teeth rattle. Then she thrusts me at Tate, who seizes a handful of my hair and drags on it. I screech, trying to duck as the flat of her hand cracks my cheek. For a split second her eyes meet mine...she's gonna kill me on the front lawn and how stupid is that?

So suddenly that I fall to my knees on the grass, Mel lets go. My head whirls, dandelions orbiting like yellow stars. Through a haze of pain, Hud Quinn's lanky body takes shape. He has Mel in a wristlock.

Hud? Coming to my rescue?

He says, "Leave Sigrid be!"

Voice sharp as an axe, Tate says, "Get lost."

"Two against one?" he says. "You got no pride?"

Mel throws her weight at him. He steps sideways, then snaps her forward so she gasps in shock. He's stronger than he looks.

I stagger upright.

Tate says, "Sigrid ratted on us."

He clicks his tongue. "Dumb as cabbages, you two.

Don't you remember Danny Grimsby's son Roy was in a dory when the tide swept him onto Knucklebones? Alls they found was bits of wood. Never found Roy. Even if she did rat you out, you should be down on your knees thanking Sigrid."

"I'm gonna call your dad," Tate says, "tell him how you broke Allan Corkum's arm last year."

Hud's face goes dead-white. There's a bruise on his jaw that stands out like a splodge of dark paint. "He broke it playing hockey on the pond!"

"You tripped him. On purpose."

"You call my dad," Hud says, "and I'll call yours. I'll ask him how you got the money for a fancy watch. You're supposed to give all your money to the Brotherhood."

Through the throbbing in my face, I watch Tate, fascinated—is she going to explode? And when is she ever speechless?

"Don't threaten me," Hud says. "You'll regret it. And leave Sigrid alone. Now git."

Tate's glaring at Hud. Hud stares back, no expression on his face. I'd give my eyeteeth, the ones that still feel loose in my jaw, to be able to do that.

"C'mon, Mel," Tate says. "No point hanging around these losers."

She's doing her best to sound tough and we all know it's not working. I'm careful not to gloat. Tate has the longest memory of anyone I know.

They walk down the path toward Tate's place.

Hud's tall for fourteen. When I crane my neck to look him in the face, the sun blinds me, too much light and all of it quivering. I waver on my feet.

He puts his hands on my shoulders and pushes down. "Head between your knees."

I'm on the grass again, and for a moment his hands stay on my shoulders. Kind of comforting, I have to say. The world settles into place.

Cautious-like, I look up. He's hunkered in front of me. His eyes don't look one bit mean. The bruise on his jaw is somewhere between purple and gray. Like storm clouds, and I'm losing it.

"Thought I was gonna pass out," I say shakily. "How did you know what to do?"

He gets to his feet, reaches down a hand. "You okay now?"

Long fingers. His nails none too clean. When I take his hand and let him pull me to my feet, his skin feels warm.

"Thanks, Hud," I mumble. "Good thing you came along."

He drops my hand. "It's not proper, girls behaving that way. Kicking. Punching."

My cheek's on fire where Tate slapped me. "If I could've gotten in a good punch, I would!"

"Punching is guy territory."

"Is that why you never bully girls—because we're wusses?"

"There's more than enough guys to whop into shape—I never get around to the girls."

"So we're not worth the trouble?"

He scratches his head. "You sure are argumentative."

"No one else at school will speak to me."

He grins, so sudden it takes me by surprise. Changes his whole face.

"Wow," I say, "you should do that more often."

The smile's wiped off like marker from the whiteboard. "You tell me what there is to smile about."

Being at the receiving end of Tate and Mel has loosened my tongue as well as my teeth. "Where'd you get that bruise on your jaw?"

"Fell off my bike." Which, I now see, is flung on the grass.

It's not the first time I've seen him with bruises. Fighting, hockey, falling off his bike, falling off his snowmobile—that's how he passes it off.

One day when Danny Grimsby was lurching along the road near my place, he told me, rum slurring his tongue, that Doyle Quinn liked using his fists on his son, Hud. But should you believe a word Danny says when he can't put one foot in front of the other?

I rub my sore nose. "You deal out plenty of crap at school and at the rink—to guys only, of course—so what you just did is totally awesome. You rescued me. Me, a girl."

Dead-serious, he says, "Put ice on your cheek and don't tell no one I rescued you. It'd ruin my reputation."

Then he heaves his bike up and takes off down the road to the wharf. Where, if Buck and Cole aren't careful, he'll toss their hockey sticks into the sea.

I watch him go. Hair greased into little spikes, him all elbows and knees, skinny as clapboard. It'll be a while before I forget how he smiled at me.

Or that he rescued me. How long since anyone rescued me from anything?

Instead of standing here feeling like I want to cry, I'd better go inside and turn the place into Fort Knox in case Tate goes on the attack again.

Sooner or later, she'll make me pay for what I just saw—her being humiliated by Hud Quinn.

EIGHT

to strive

I put a bag of ice to my cheek soon as I get home. I follow this with a light coat of my mother's liquid foundation, then blusher on the good side of my face to balance things off.

My mother stayed here the last two nights, although both times she arrived after I went to sleep and left before the school bus. As for Lorne, he's mostly eating at Sally's after work, and he's got bags under his eyes because of the late hours he's keeping. I figure he's in love.

Seal lands home for supper today, third day in a row. I wish it was because he wants to, and not because he's doing the heavy in place of my real father.

I start serving the meat loaf, boiled potatoes, and string beans.

Hud's a bit like a string bean.

Tall. My real dad was tall.

Is tall.

For the last seven years, he's lived in Fort McMurray, which I picture as one big mother of a Newfoundland outport excepting there's no ocean. He writes to me and

Lorne once a month, and once a month I write back. I talk about the weather, my marks in school, the new manager at FoodMart. I sign them, *your loving daughter, Sigrid.* Oh yeah, and I say *thank you,* because every month there's a crisp, red fifty-dollar bill in my envelope. Lorne's, too.

He's never once come home for a visit.

He told me early last year he'd moved in with a woman called Barb who has two kids, four and five. You can imagine how that made me feel. Or maybe you can't.

The money comes in handy.

Seal says mildly, "Sigrid, dinner's getting cold."

My cheeks turn pink. Seems mingy to be thinking about my real dad when Seal's the one keeping me company in the kitchen. I put the plates on the table and we sit down, me with my back to the light.

Seal picks up his knife and fork. "Did you steer clear of Tate and Mel today?"

"Didn't speak a word to them." Whimpers and yelps don't count.

"Are you making any new friends?"

"I don't need friends."

"We all need friends."

"I got a rep, Seal! Hanging around with Tate and Mel didn't make me Miss Popularity."

He nails me with his blue eyes. "But you're never gonna hang around with them again, right?"

"No way," I say, and believe me, I sound sincere.

"Then all you have to do is get the word out."

"It's not that simple. Not when you've been a Shrike for two years."

"Bullying," Seal says, chewing his meat loaf like it's the toughest of steaks.

"There's reasons no one at school will speak to me. Good reasons."

He takes another forkful. "Then you gotta change their minds."

"How?"

"Dunno."

"Me, either."

He pokes at his potatoes. "Start small, I guess."

If this was anyone but Seal, I'd go ballistic. "Okay, let's talk about friends. You remember Hanna? She was my best friend, my only friend, from when I was four years old. We were like sisters...we didn't need anyone else. But when I was ten, she moved away. To Calgary. Other side of the country. We still text and sometimes we Skype—but not near as often as we used to because it isn't the same."

One reason it isn't the same is because I've never told Hanna I turned into a Shrike. If she found out, she'd cut me off at the knees. Then, to make it worse, when she asked if I had any new friends, I lied to her. *Prinny's my new friend,* that's what I told her.

"Seal," I say, and to my dismay, my voice breaks, "how will I ever find another Hanna?"

He pats my hand.

We eat dessert, store-bought apple pie. We put away the leftovers. We do the dishes. But in all that time, he doesn't come up with an answer.

Thursday morning while I'm getting dressed, I'm still hearing the echo of Seal's voice in my ears. *We all need friends...*

Me more than most, I'm starting to think. So should I give it a try?

Hanna and me were tight, so it's not like I never had a friend. And it'll give me something to think about besides Tate and Mel.

The rest of the day I smile at everyone who crosses my path.

Not a single kid smiles back, or speaks to me on the bus, in school, at recess, or in the cafeteria. This includes Hud, who doesn't even make eye contact. It's like he never rescued me.

After school, Mr. Murphy waits for me to reach the front door of my place before he puts the bus in gear. Quickly I lock the doors and windows. Then I sit on my bed and think hard about this friendship deal. It's turning into a challenge. Okay, so smiling didn't work. What can I try next?

If I had a proper mother, I could ask her advice. But she's gone again, off to an estate sale in the Humber Valley with Ady. Ady, her best friend.

Friday morning, I tuck two cards in my backpack. One is a get-well card with a spray of pink and blue flowers on the front, the other a misty green landscape with a road wandering into the distance and *Bon Voyage* across the top. I wouldn't mind driving my bike along that road and disappearing around the bend.

I signed each card, *Sincerely, Sigrid Sugden.*

The first one is for Nicole Greene. Her dad is the town lawyer and for sure the Shrikes never bullied her. Nicole thinks she's better than the rest of us and lots of kids don't like her; but her dad has cancer, and that has to be rough. If I think of Seal getting sick…

When the bell rings for recess, I head for her desk, holding out the card in its pretty blue envelope. "This is for you and your dad," I say. "I hope you like it."

Nicole has a classy haircut and wears eye make-up to school. She looks at me, looks at the card, and takes it with the very tips of her fingers.

"Move along there, girls," Mrs. Dooks says.

I hurry for the door. I thought she'd say *thank you,* which would be two more words than anyone's spoken to me all morning. Outside, as usual, I lean against the wall near Mr. Marsden. As Nicole saunters past with her best friend, Joan Bidson, the mayor's daughter, Nicole hands the card to Joan, saying loudly, "Who does she think she is, poking her nose into my family?"

"She's from the cove—you wouldn't expect her to understand," Joan says.

Nicole drops the card on the pavement. Joan steps on it. Then the wind picks it up. The flowers flutter. There's dirt on them from Joan's shoe.

When the teacher's looking the other way, I dart forward, grab the card, bend it in two, and jam it in the pocket of my jeans. My fingers are trembling.

I hope no one else noticed.

I almost chicken out for the second card.

C'mon, Sigrid, you can do this...

At lunchtime, before we head for the cafeteria, I take the other card, which has a pale green envelope, and hold it out to Kim Corkum, who's moving from Long Bight with her family to—you got it—Alberta. Kim is a cousin of Mel's. Can't imagine she'll miss Mel.

Kim says suspiciously, "What's that?"

"It's a card for you," I say, "because you're moving."

"No, thanks," she says and turns her back on me.

Nicole is whispering something to Joan, who giggles

out loud. Other kids are eyeing me curiously. My cheeks flame.

I scoot back to my desk, shove the card in my pack, and stand at the very end of the line-up for the cafeteria.

NINE

to repay

Seal isn't coming home for supper; he told me ahead of time, with one of his heavy-duty can-I-trust-you looks. I can't stand being in the house one more minute with the dingy curtains and dust bunnies in the living room, the dirty dishes in the kitchen, the floor that needs scrubbing. Mel got off the bus in Long Bight. I check through every window to see if Tate's hanging around before I sneak out of the kitchen through the glass doors. On the barrens a bird is singing, sharp as a whistle, like it knows what life's all about and it feels just fine, thank-you-very-much. I scurry through the side door of the garage, haul my bike outdoors, look both ways again, then head west, toward Long Bight and St. Fabien. I don't have a plan. But I'll go stir-crazy if I sit home from now until dark.

It feels good to be pumping my bike up the hills and coasting down them. The wind on my face blows away Nicole's snippiness, Kim's rejection, all those catty giggles. You're bound to run into some snags when you try to change your ways. Only natural.

My bike veers onto the shoulder. So that's what I'm

doing? Trying to change my ways?

Of course I am. And past due, I'd say.

I pedal up a hill, and it's as if the blood pulsing through my veins clears my brain; the thoughts tumble out, one after the other. For the first ten years of my life, I was a good girl, a nice girl—and where did that get me? My real dad in Fort McMurray, my mother at Ady's, and Hanna in Calgary, that's where. *Nice?* I was sick of *nice.* And then Tate Cody started paying attention to me. Sure, I had a smartphone and money for places like McDonald's and Subway. But more than that, I was angry and I was desperate. Tate's smart—she knew I'd jump at the chance to become a Shrike.

I never chose the victims. That was Tate's job. And I was never the heavy, I left that to Mel. Trouble is, once my *mean* was all used up, I grew more and more ashamed of what we were doing.

But I kept right on doing it.

Last Friday was a breakthrough. Last Friday gave me the chance to *change my situation,* just like Mr. MacInney said.

If I could only figure out how.

I wander the aisles at Walmart. For some reason our dingy living-room curtains are stuck in my craw. It's amazing how cheap new curtains can be. I pick up a package of gold sheers, then put them down again. My mother wouldn't stoop to buying curtains at Walmart. They'd have to be from some highfalutin outlet on the Shopping Channel.

Not that she's interested enough in our place—or in Seal, Lorne, or me—to buy anything for the house. Fancy clothes and a splashy car, that's where she spends her money.

I go in search of toothpaste. Which is when I catch sight of Vi Dunston at the opposite end of the aisle, slipping a bar of soap into her jacket pocket.

I turn away, fast. I'll never forget the first time I saw her shoplifting...

← ← ←
↖ ↖

My two-month anniversary as a Shrike had just passed, and I was riding high. Tate, Mel, and me were at the mall, after school on a Thursday; they wanted to go to the video store, but I needed some wrapping paper, so I told them I'd meet them in a few minutes and ran to the Dollar Store.

Vi was in the third aisle, out of sight of the cash registers, standing in front of a display of plastic hair grips and elastics. Without even thinking, I took out my smartphone and waited; when she shoved a bundle of elastics into her jacket pocket, I clicked the picture.

Yep. Perfect.

I crept up the aisle toward her. "Hello, Vi."

She froze like a deer caught in a car's headlights; then her hand slid down to cover her pocket.

What an amateur. "Doing a little shopping?" I said.

"I gotta go."

"I'm done here, too. Let's leave together."

No shouts, no alarms, no security guy on our heels. Once we were two stores down, I gripped her by the arm, steering her toward the nearest bench. "Sit a minute, Vi."

She tried to wriggle free. "Can't—I'm late!"

My fingers biting into her flesh, me smiling the whole time so it looked like two friends having a nice visit, I eased her down on the bench. "So you like elastics in your hair, do you?"

Never much color in her cheeks, but right then they were a good match for my white t-shirt. She started chewing her nails.

"Freebies are fun, are they, Vi?"

She's made her cuticle bleed. Pathetic. Why didn't she fight back? Show some spunk? "If you're gonna shoplift, at least take something worthwhile."

"I didn't—"

I hauled out my phone and showed her the photo.

"What did you do that for?" she whispered.

Because I'm mad at the world and I'm taking it out on you.

"Tate'll be interested in seeing it, don't you think? Mel, too."

"No..."

"Should be worth twenty bucks, minimum."

Two tears dripped down her cheeks. I didn't want the other shoppers guessing what I was up to, so I put my phone away. "We'll be in touch. Start saving your money, Vi—you don't want Mel on your case."

I drew my finger across my throat, smiled at her, and walked away.

We got thirty bucks out of her that time.

I hurry out of Walmart without the toothpaste, shame and guilt squirming in my belly. How could I have been so mean to a hopeless case like Vi?

Not just mean. Enjoying being mean.

My feet have brought me to the bank where I keep my money in a savings account. I stare at my reflection in the big plate-glass window.

Fifty dollars a month has a habit of adding up because Seal pays for my clothes. And, of course, I made money as a Shrike. *Twenty dollars or we'll rough up your little sister. Forty dollars or we'll post that photo online.* Give

Tate her due, after she took her fifty percent cut, she always gave me and Mel twenty-five percent each.

My share from Vi and the elastics? $7.50.

This spring, we squeezed a lot of bucks out of Prinny after we got her drunk on vodka at my place. The photos of her mother sloshed at the club didn't hurt, either.

I stare at the bank machine like I never saw one before.

I know how I can change my ways. How I can make amends for all the bad stuff I was part of.

Pulling out my bank card, I punch my code and hit the button for Withdraw Cash. How much cash is the question? I settle on eighty bucks.

After treating myself to a cheeseburger at McDonald's, which breaks up one of the twenties, I head out of town, keeping a weather eye for Mel at the Long Bight turnoff and for Tate in Fiddlers Cove. By the time I reach Ratchet, I'm out of breath. Prinny's house looks some different since they painted it. The door is a deep green, and there's flowers planted out front.

My heart's thumping, and it's not just from the bike ride. Using the new brass knocker, I rap on the door.

"C'mon in," Prinny's father hollers.

I walk through the front porch into the kitchen. The tablecloth has yellow daffodils all over it, the walls look freshly painted, and the cupboards are new, too, a smooth, pale wood. Prinny's da raises his face from the newspaper. "Oh," he says, "it's you. What can I do for you?"

"Hello, Sigrid," Prinny's ma says, from where she's standing by the sink.

"Um...is Prinny home, please?"

"She's over to Laice's."

Despite all the new-looking stuff, the kitchen's right homey, as if the people who live in it are happy to be there. "Thanks," I say.

Laice Hadden has been staying with her grandparents, Mattie and Starald, because her parents are divorcing. Her and Prinny are tight, like me and Hanna used to be.

Mattie's garden is sprinkled with shrubs and plaster gnomes, the grass a dense green. Not one dandelion. I contemplate biking home, doing this tomorrow. Or never.

I ring the bell.

Mattie opens the door. The smell of fresh-baked cookies tickles my nose. She smiles at me, wiping her hands on her apron. "Can I help you, dear?"

"I'm looking for Prinny."

"She's with Laice in the bedroom. Come right this way."

I shuck off my sneakers because it's that kind of house, cross the thick, beige carpet in the living room, noticing frilly curtains at the windows, and magazines neatly lined up on the coffee table. I don't bother searching for dust bunnies. One look at Mattie and they'd be on the fly.

She taps on the bedroom door. "You have a visitor, Laice," Mattie says, beams at me, and goes back to the kitchen.

When Laice sees it's me, she half-closes the door, stationing herself in the gap.

Pretty doesn't cut it when it comes to Laice Hadden. She's so beautiful she could be a model. She says, throwing her words over her shoulder, "Prinny, it's Sigrid."

As Prinny comes to the door, I glimpse more frilly curtains, pink and white, and a white-painted bed with a pink spread. I take my wallet from my pack, hold out fifty dollars, and say in a rush, "I quit being a Shrike, Prinny. So I'm giving you back my share of the money we took."

"I don't want it," she says.

I remember how Nicole dropped my card in the dirt, how Kim refused to even touch the envelope. My heart stutters in my chest. "But it's your money!"

"Give it to the animal shelter in St. Fabien," she says. "Or to Dr. Larkin, the vet—her clinic has a fund for stray cats."

My face heats up like someone flicked a switch on the stove. Me, Tate, and Mel let Prinny's two cats outdoors last spring, and one of them got lost on the barrens. Took until the next day for Prinny to find him.

I was the one who dropped them out the window.

I back up, hurry across the living room, thrust my feet into my sneaks, and I'm out the door. After jumping a flowerbed, I run across the lawn and pedal away as if fifty stray cats are yowling at my heels.

TEN

to scour

When I pad into the kitchen in my bare feet the next morning, Seal's standing by the window. His shoulders are slumped and he's frowning so deep that for a minute he looks like a stranger.

I accidentally-on-purpose bang my hip against the table. He jumps. Looks at me as though I'm the stranger.

My mother was home last night. Is that what's wrong?

"You okay?" I say uncertainly.

"Yeah...yeah, I'm fine. You want to do groceries later this morning?"

"Whenever."

"Think I'll mow the lawn," he says and he hurries out like there's grass sprouting between his toes.

I pour some cereal, chew it like it's pebbles, and make a list. He's done the dishes—sink empty, counters wiped. I feel a twinge of guilt. We divvy up the kitchen chores, the two of us, because Lorne and my mother don't do chores; lately I haven't been carrying my part of the load. I rinse out my bowl, wipe it dry, and put it in the cupboard. *Dish soap,* I write on the list.

The whole way to St. Fabien, Seal doesn't say a word. When we reach the vet clinic, I ask if he'll drop me off and I'll catch up with him at FoodMart in ten minutes. He gives me a blank look. "Sure," he says.

My chest sore, I jump down and watch him drive away. Then I walk up the path to the clinic. It's already busy: cats in cages, dogs on leashes, their owners stroking and patting them. Drool running from one dog's jaws; a cat mewling like a sick baby.

"Little diddums, poor little diddums," one lady is saying to a pint-size dog whose face is squashed into a permanent snarl.

I'd pictured myself and the vet having this cosy chat, just the two of us.

I walk up to the front desk where the receptionist, whose name tag says Colleen, is scowling at her computer. She transfers the scowl to my face. "Yes?"

"Is the vet in? Dr. Larkin?"

"She's booked solid until 3:25."

Colleen hits a button and the printer whirs. I say, over the noise, "I want to make a donation."

That gets her attention. "What kind of donation?"

"For stray cats."

"How much?"

I take the bills out of my pocket, smoothing them flat. "Fifty dollars."

"That's a lot of money for someone your age."

"I saved it up," I say, which is a complicated mix of truth and lies.

"I'd have to check with Dr. Larkin to see if we're allowed to take donations from minors," she says. "Take a seat."

"I can't stay."

"Then come back on a weekday when the regular receptionist is here."

I turn around. Customers are staring at me. As I beat a retreat, Little Diddums growls.

Colleen's scowl should be posted online. In her spare time, I bet she kicks puppies. I bet she dumps kittens on the side of the road.

You shoved two cats out a window...remember?

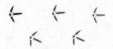

Seal and me whip along the aisles at FoodMart in record time. Only person we meet is Mr. Corkum, Mel's dad. He's a big guy with stooped shoulders and eyes sadder than a chained dog. He looks at Seal and Seal looks at him. Neither one smiles.

Mr. Corkum picks up a box of All Bran. I pick up a box of Weetabix. Then we're past each other.

Mel's mother was a big, cheerful woman who wore bush pants, and earrings made of peacock feathers; she used to drive eighteen-wheelers. She wasn't home much, but when she was, you could hear her laugh all the way from Long Bight to Fiddlers Cove. Her truck jackknifed in a snowstorm on the 401. We went to the wake. Everyone along the shore did because she acted the same no matter if you were Danny Grimsby in his cups or the mayor in his fancy suit.

Mel's dad changed after she died. Closed right down. And Mel turned into Tate's muscleman.

Seeing him makes me feel right heavy; I don't have the heart to try the animal shelter today. So after we've loaded the groceries in the truck, we drive straight home. Lorne's car is gone because he's doing his Saturday stint at the garage.

The lawnmower clipped off all the dandelions.

Seal helps me carry in the plastic bags. "Guess I'll have a shower."

I put away the groceries. When he comes out, he's wearing his best jeans and a new shirt with blue and white stripes, a blue that matches his eyes. He says, "You got plans for the rest of the day?"

"Maybe I'll rake the lawn."

"That'd be good. You're staying clear of Mel and Tate?"

"Looks like you've got plans," I say.

He looks anywhere but at me. "Yeah…guess I'll head out. Your mother's taken off again, back the first of the week. But I won't be late, and you can call me on my cell if you need anything."

"Okay," I say, but I'm saying it to myself because he's

already gone. I'd bet my fifty dollars I know where he's going and it's not Tim Hortons and the reason he was so edgy this morning is because he's nursing a guilty conscience for dating Davina Murphy.

So here I am at 11:45 on a Saturday morning with nothing to do. Normally, all three of us Shrikes would be in town casing the mall—Tate amusing herself with a bit of shoplifting, Mel getting in the occasional kick at a kid whose mother's attention has wandered, me eyeing the racks of jeans and tops.

A Snickers bar—that's what I need. I go into the pantry, where I stashed all the new stuff in front of the old. The box of Snickers is way at the back and suddenly I'm so mad I can hardly breathe.

The pantry's a mess.

The house is a mess.

My whole life is a mess.

So what am I going to do, stand here gawping at a box of Snickers?

I start turfing stuff onto the floor: cereal boxes, canned beans and corn and peas, double-chocolate cookies for Lorne, Tostitos for Seal, plastic bottles of ketchup, mustard, and relish. The shelf needs a good scrub. I head for the sink, dump the contents of the blue plastic bucket on the kitchen floor, and fill the bucket with pine cleanser and hot water. Lots of rags under the sink, and first thing you know I'm scouring the shelf as though my whole messed-up life depends on it.

I used too much cleanser. The pantry's gonna stink of pine.

I empty the next shelf and by the time I've scrubbed it, the first one is dry. *Okay, Sigrid, you need a system.*

I dump another shelf, scrub, then start lining up the cans and boxes, veggies here, fruit next to it, cookies together, cereal on the top shelf. I check expiry dates, bring out a garbage bag, throw out stale Ritz crackers and some powdered milk from five years ago. Five *years?*

Last thing I tackle is the floor. The scrub brush does wonders. The floor is pretty, little green flecks in swirls of beige. So if the floor has green in it, why do we have pink curtains on the kitchen windows?

By the time I finish the pantry, I'm out of breath and my arm aches. I dump the dirty water down the sink, rinse the bucket, wring out the rag, and then I stand at the door of the pantry and admire it. So neat. So orderly. I adjust a package of cereal, restack the cans of corn. The first guy to make a mess in here, Lorne or Seal, will get an earful.

Where I left off scrubbing the floor, there's a line, pale beige with green swirls on one side, dark beige with the green hardly showing on the other.

I eat lunch at the kitchen table, and the whole time that line is pulling my eyes.

The pink curtains hang limp at the windows.

I push back from the table.

I go through all the kitchen cupboards, throwing out chipped plates and glasses and non-stick fry pans so old and scratchy that everything sticks, including cooking oil and dust.

Wipe the shelves, stack everything real tidy.

Pull down the curtains, bundle them into the garbage.

Windex the glass.

Scrub months of grease spots off the kettle and coffee pot.

Look into the oven, shudder, and close it.

Call Lorne on his cell, tell him to bring home oven cleaner and rubber gloves, *don't ask questions, just do it, and you're taking me to Walmart, I don't care if you've got a date.*

Measure the clean windows.

Spray the oven as soon as Lorne comes home.

Listen to him complain all the way to town.

Buy new curtains, dish rack, dish cloths, dish towels, hand towels, and oven gloves, using his credit card.

Don't answer when he asks what I'm doing because I don't have a clue.

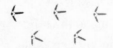

By nine p.m., the green swirls on the beige kitchen floor

are picking up the green leaves in the crisp, off-white kitchen curtains. A green towel is hanging on the rail of the shiny-clean oven. A green cloth is folded neatly on the new white sink tray. The table and chairs gleam with lemon oil.

I look down at myself. Oven cleaner on my shirt, knees of my jeans stained gray, hands reeking of pine and lemon, and every muscle aching.

Just as well Lorne went to Sally's for supper and Seal didn't come home. I wish I had the energy to stay up and see Seal's face, but already I'm yawning. I leave him a note by the front door.

Hi, Seal! Shoes off before you go into the kitchen!! Don't make a mess!!! Luv, Sigrid.

Luv, Sigrid...

ELEVEN

to remember

In the morning when I go into the kitchen, Seal's already up. Guiltily, he wipes a few coffee grains from the counter.

"Looks right nice, Sigrid."

"I bought some new stuff with Lorne's credit card. I hope that's okay."

Something flickers in his eyes. "Sure," he says, "it's okay. Long overdue. How about I cook supper tonight?"

"Just don't spill anything on the floor," I say, and we both laugh.

Was I cleaning the kitchen so he could see I'm trustworthy?

Maybe so, because right after breakfast—he does the dishes with the nice new cloth—he takes off. Doesn't say where he's going.

When he doesn't trust me, he stays home being a stepdad and looking grumpy. When he does, he disappears.

I have a shower in our dingy bathroom, which has a faded gray mat and no two towels the same color.

Sunday is the one day of the week I'm safe from Tate,

so I take my bike out of the garage. I'm not going near Walmart; I ride east toward Gulley Cove again. The wind's off the sea, smelling of salt—not a whiff of oven cleaner—and the sky is a clear, fresh blue like it's just been rinsed and hung out to dry.

Being on a bike doesn't use your scrubbing muscles.

I come level with Abe Murphy's. His truck's not in the yard, nor is his dog. On impulse, I leave my bike leaning against his fence and walk up the path to the barn. The cow in the field eyes me, chewing thoughtful-like, flicking flies with her tail. Her coat is light brown, clean, and shiny. I better not get hooked on that word *clean*.

The barn door creaks open. I catch a flash of white and see a cat leap from the floor and scale five bales of hay to the loft. He stands on the crossbeam, tail thrashing, eyes huge. I overheard Prinny and Travis talking on the bus one day about a cat called Ghost who no one can tame and who lives in the barn.

"Hello, Ghost," I say.

The cat vanishes into the shadows of the loft. A chicken hops up the wooden ramp into a wire pen equipped with water and food dishes, all nicely topped up. There's a pig in a roomy enclosure, and he's clean, too. He grunts at me.

Mel's lashes are near as light as the pig's. I wonder what she's up to today.

Carefully, I close the latch on the barn door and walk

down the path beside a garden where potatoes and peas are already poking up.

Picking up my bike, I wander across the road and stare out to sea. If Abe knew I shoved two cats out the window, he wouldn't be too happy with me visiting his barn.

There was a nor'easter that afternoon, the rain pouring down, wind battering the houses, and it's like I'm back there, back at Prinny's place with Tate and Mel...

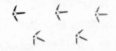

Lorne had driven the three of us there right after school, on a day that Prinny was visiting Laice. We told Lorne we had some books to deliver. Lied to him.

Lorne isn't the type to tell lies. So he trusts what you tell him.

Because the front door was locked, we hurried around to the back of the house, where someone had left a window open. "In you go, Sigrid," Tate said.

She knew I didn't want to do this. Added to her enjoyment, that's the way I saw it. I levered the window higher and clambered over the sill. Mel hoisted Tate up. She landed with a small thump on the floor.

We were in a room with a washer and dryer, clothes hampers, and four old wooden chairs in need of a coat of paint. "Move," Tate said, "we ain't got all day."

I followed her down the hall to the kitchen, which was

very clean and stank of Javex. A ginger cat was curled up neat as could be on the cushion of an old rocking chair. "Grab it," she said.

I bent over and picked the cat up. She—I was sure it was a she—didn't weigh as much as I'd expected; her fur was silky smooth. She eyed me lazily, yawned, showing her pink throat, and butted her head against my arm. Then she started purring.

"Sigrid! Get a move on."

Carrying the cat as gently as I could, I hurried back down the hall. "Out the window," Tate said.

"But it's raining!"

"Do it," she said in her quiet voice, the one that turns my spine to ice.

I leaned as far over the sill as I could, and let go of the cat real careful. Mel kicked at it. With a piercing meow, it streaked toward the shed and darted underneath.

It was out of the rain. And it was safe from Mel. Maybe this wouldn't be so bad after all.

Tate was calling from another room. "The other cat's in here."

She was in Prinny's bedroom. Nothing fancy—reminded me of my own bedroom. The second cat, who was gray with four white paws and a guy kind of jaw, reared his head up, his body tense.

I gotta do this. I gotta.

I quickly gathered him in my arms. He hissed at me,

the centers of his eyes like black discs. When he wriggled, I almost lost him. Clutching him around the middle, him squirming and yowling, I ran down the hall. As I lifted him to the window, he snagged my wrist with his claws and dug them in.

"Ouch!"

Mel was backed against the house, sheltering from the rain. I dropped the cat and he landed on all fours. Mel lunged at him. He bolted away from the house straight for the nearest shrubs.

Straight for the barrens.

"Help me out the window!" Tate said.

I gave her a knee-up, and scrambled over the windowsill right behind her. The ground jarred my ankles. The wind was howling like fifty feral cats.

When I slammed the car door and shook the rain from my jacket, Lorne said, "Took you long enough."

If he knew what I just did…I pulled my sleeve over the punctures in my wrist, where blood was oozing.

The warmth of the cats' bodies, the way their ribs curved under my palm….

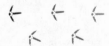

The wind—a gentle summer wind—is playing with my hair. I climb on my bike and pedal along the dirt road toward Gulley Cove, listening to the waves smash against the cliffs. I hate remembering that day. Of all the nasty things I did as a Shrike, dropping Prinny's cats out the window into a nor'easter was by far the worst.

The meanest. The most cowardly. No wonder Prinny wouldn't take my fifty dollars.

Maybe I should go home and curl up in a ball on my bedspread.

Then, around the bend, who do I see but Hud.

He's sitting at the cliff's edge, staring out to sea. More than staring. It's like he's already out there, his whole body leaning into the horizon.

The spokes of his bike catch the sun.

My tires hit a rut, rasping in the dirt. He gives a start and turns his head, shading his eyes. When he sees me, his shoulders hunch. Couldn't say *go away* more clearly than if he hollered it.

I lay my bike down next to his, sit beside him on another rock, and gaze out to sea. There's comfortable silences—me and Seal can do those—and there's the other kind that scream at you. My nerves tighten. "What are you up to?"

"Minding my own business."

"Tate and Mel haven't bothered me since."

"So why don't you quit bothering me!"

I bite my lip. There's a nasty scrape down the side of his face and the question is out before I can stop it. "Your dad do that to you?"

Face like a fist, Hud says, "Lay off."

"Danny Grimsby told me your dad beats up on you."

"Danny's nuthin' but a no-account drunk."

Hud surges to his feet, throws his leg over his bike, and takes off in the direction of Gulley Cove. Looks kind of comical, knees bent sideways on his pitiful excuse for a bicycle.

I'm not smiling.

Twelve

to criticize

All the flavor's gone from the day. Even Hud Quinn and a scruffy barn cat run the other way when they see me; and I can't get Prinny's cats out of my mind. I slouch into the house.

Lorne left dirty dishes in the sink and crumbs on the counter.

He's in his room, music blaring from his old boom box. This only happens when he's in a good mood. I bang on the door.

"Yeah?"

Bed not made, him in his boxers looking like a cat who's feasted on tuna. I announce, "You're taking me to town this afternoon."

"Says who?"

"And from now on, do your own dishes!"

"You're not my mother!"

For a moment we're both silent. Then his lips twitch and so do mine. "No, Lorne, I'm not your mother. Seal will pay you for what you spent yesterday, and your limit can cover some new stuff for the bathroom, right?"

Easy to see where this is going. By eight o'clock that night the bathroom's done. Clean floor, tub shining. Jazzy gray shower curtain splashed with red flowers. New towels, red and dark gray. A red bathmat and tank cover, and a cute red ceramic soap dish.

I pin a list of rules on the door.

Next morning, brushing my teeth in the red and gray bathroom, taking my cereal box from the tidy row of boxes, wiping the counter with the new green cloth... maybe I should give *nice* another go at school today. Time's passed and surely the kids can see I'm not hanging with Tate and Mel anymore.

On the bus, I smile at Hud, who doesn't smile back. Then I sit down beside the Herbey girls. "Hi," I say, real pleasant, "what did you do all weekend?"

Taylor ignores me. Brianna giggles.

Tate says, "Sigrid, no one wants to spend the time of day with you."

We'll see about that.

In class, I smile at Prinny, Laice, Travis, Hector, Cole, Buck, Avery, Kim, and Beth-Anne. Travis nods. Hector grunts. Otherwise, eyes slide away from me and backs are turned.

At recess, I stand on the outskirts of a group around

Nicole and Joan. They all snub me. In the cafeteria, I sit down with Shirl and Sarah. They get up and move.

I stay put, sitting all by myself. Once again, *nice* isn't working. The kids don't trust me, and who can blame them?

I dig at the crust on my sandwich with my fingernail. No one's going to be my friend. Bad enough that I was a Shrike. But all those years when Hanna and me were best friends, we ignored the other kids because we didn't need them—we had each other. So why, just because I want them to, should the kids start cozying up to me now?

I need a change of strategy.

Making amends, that's the route to go. Okay, so it didn't work with Prinny, but that's likely because I started with the worst case first.

As I'm walking back to our classroom after lunch, I see Avery Quinn with his head stuck in his locker. I take twenty dollars from my wallet. "Avery," I say.

He flinches and turns around, not looking at me. "Yeah?"

I hold out a twenty-dollar bill. "This is my share of the money we took from you because of that photo."

He blushes scarlet. What kid wants a photo of nose-picking posted online? I stick the bill between his fingers. "I'm right sorry," I say and walk away before he can hand the money back.

One down, one to go.

I catch nail-biter Vi Dunston on her way to the bus. "I want you to take this," I say, thrusting another twenty at her. "I'm real sorry about the photo I took."

She looks just as scared taking the money as she did when we were threatening her. I climb the steps of the bus, sit by myself, and stare out the window.

Question is, do I feel any better?

Ashamed is how I feel. Deep down ashamed.

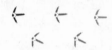

That night, I clean my bedroom. I have to change the bag in the vacuum cleaner after it sucked up the dust bunnies under the bed. What would Hanna think of all this cleaning? Missing her—the lowdown ache I carried around, day after day—it's mostly gone now. But when she left, the playfulness, the dancing in me, got sucked right out.

Being a Shrike took their place.

Lying to Hanna took their place.

I stand still, the hose looped at my feet. Lies are a worse problem than the 5000 kilometers of highway between Fiddlers Cove and Calgary.

Have I ever admitted that before?

Around nine-thirty, the front door opens and shuts. Thinking it's Seal, I wander out in my PJs. It's not Seal, it's my mother.

"Ady's TV on the fritz?" I say.

"Don't be lippy. I need a mug-up."

She stops dead at the kitchen door, me on her heels. "Who did this?" she says.

"Me."

"New dish towels? Nothing wrong with the old ones. And where's my pink curtains?"

"In the garbage."

"Your dad and me bought those curtains when you were born!"

"Yeah, and I'm nearly thirteen."

Hands on her hips, cheeks flushed, she rounds on me. "You don't run this house."

For some stupid reason, I thought she'd like what I did. "Neither do you. Not all the way from Ady's."

"Where's Seal?"

"Out."

She pours water into the shiny kettle, slopping it down the sides. "Don't you go making any more changes around here, girl."

"Past time somebody did something. You'd better check the bathroom."

She storms into the bathroom and storms back out again. "This stuff you been buying—you sure didn't go for quality. And who's paying for it?"

"Lorne. So far."

"Both of you, going behind my back." She opens the nearest cupboard, squawks in dismay. "My mug, my blue mug—"

"It was chipped. From the dishwasher."

"You're not to touch one more thing in this house!"

"I'll do what I want!"

My turn to storm out of the kitchen. I slam my bedroom door and throw myself down on my bedspread. I wish I lived in Fort McMurray. I wish I lived anywhere in the world except Fiddlers Cove, Newfoundland.

In the living room, the TV's blaring. But she turns it off at 11 p.m. and the house goes quiet.

It's midnight before Seal parks his truck in the driveway. If he really is dating Davina Murphy, tongues'll be wagging from Ratchet to St. Fabien, enough tongues to drown out the Shopping Channel and eBay. Did my mother come home to check up on him?

Although I listen hard, I don't hear voices from their bedroom, easy-going voices or angry ones. All I hear is the toilet flush, then the creak of springs in the couch. So that's where Seal's sleeping.

Misery sits on my chest heavier than Abe's pig.

How much longer will Seal last? And why did I rip the

kitchen apart? It made him and Lorne nervous as the white cat, and my mother explode like a firecracker.

Never in a hundred years will I understand my mother.

Thirteen

to decide

My mother's mood isn't improved when she discovers Seal's already left for Tim Hortons by the time she gets up.

The cushions on the couch have been smoothed flat.

She says, fastening a braided leather belt around her waist, "We'll be in Roddickton the next while—an aunt of Ady's died and left a houseful of stuff. Tell Seal I'll likely be back Friday."

"Okay," I say, and disappear to get dressed.

On the bus, as we slow down for the school driveway, Tate says loudly, "Sigrid, did you know Seal's truck was parked in Davina Murphy's driveway again last evening? You better start hunting for a new stepdad."

Inside me, something snaps. "I'd rather have six stepdads than a father who wouldn't crack a smile if God Himself moved to Fiddlers Cove!"

She's on her feet and I am, too. Mr. Murphy says, "Sit down, girls! The bus is still moving."

We both sit down. She looks murderous. I scowl

through the window, trying to calm down. I didn't bother smiling at anyone on the bus this morning. At least kids noticed me when I was a Shrike; now they don't pay me any heed at all. Which is worse, to have kids afraid of you or acting like you're invisible?

The morning grinds by. I keep my head down. In history class Mr. Marsden—who, even though he's a teacher, sometimes says interesting things—mentions that short men are often aggressive: Napoleon, Alexander the Great, and the dictator in North Korea with the pouffy hairdo who died a while ago. *Overcompensating*, he says. So is that why Tate bullies, because she's short?

I rub the seam flat on my scribbler. Making someone feel smaller makes you feel bigger. As one of the Shrikes, I was Somebody. I wasn't a girl whose best friend moved away. I wasn't a daughter whose father upped and left, and whose mother is never home so how can she leave? I was one-third of Tate-Mel-and-Sigrid.

The noon bell shrills in the hallway. Books slam shut, chairs scrape. Mr. Marsden shouts, "Test on Friday. Don't forget to study."

I lag behind. I'm in no hurry to sit by myself in the cafeteria.

Would Tate take me back?

After me sassing her on the bus this morning? Not likely.

To be a Shrike again—that's not really what I want, is it?

But if Tate and Mel were on my side again, there'd be no more checking over my shoulder every move I make. No more asking Mr. Murphy to wait by the side of the road until I'm in the front door. No more cracks about Davina and Seal.

It feels like the walls are closing in on me, the air so stale I can scarce breathe. I could go to the office, pleading a headache, and ask the secretary to call Lorne to drive me home.

Won't solve anything. Same deal tomorrow.

I trudge down the hallway to the cafeteria. Then I stop so fast I'm teetering on my toes. Just outside the cafeteria, Selena Greene is backed against the wall, Mel looming over her. Tate's to one side, her cruel smile, her empty eyes.

So much for Tate and Mel being forbidden to hang out together.

Selena's crying. Not a teacher to be seen as she brings her fist from behind her back, opens it, and drops some coins into Tate's outstretched hand.

If I was a Shrike again, I'd be standing right behind Tate, phone at the ready in case there's a photo op.

You disappoint me, Sigrid...

Four steps close the gap. With the flat of my hand, I knock the coins out of Tate's hand. As they roll across the tiles, Mel thumps her big foot over them.

"You that hard up, Tate Cody," I say, "that you have to steal quarters from a kid in grade two? How's Selena supposed to buy lunch?"

"Worrying about a kid's lunch never stopped you before."

She's right.

The anger of months erupts from my chest. "You've got no decency at all, you or your pig-faced enforcer. Take your foot off that money, Mel Corkum, right now!"

Someone gasps. Someone else giggles, a nervous giggle. A small crowd of kids is watching. Hud's ambling toward us. He doesn't do anything, just stands there behind the rest of them.

Not one of them doing anything. Not one of them. My fists clench at my sides. "Mel, did you hear me?"

Mel moves her sneaker.

I pick up a loonie and three quarters, pitiful really, given the prices in the cafeteria; then I glue my eyes to Mel's. "You should hang around with someone else."

"Like who?" Tate snaps.

"Tate, anyone in this school would be an improvement on you."

She steps forward. I stand my ground.

Hud says, right easy, "Mr. Marsden's coming down the hall."

As I glance that way, Tate rips a fist into my belly. I

double over and the coins fly to the floor again. She brushes off her knuckles. "You better watch your back as well as your mouth, Sigrid. Now stand up straight so we'll be spared embarrassing questions."

Automatically, I obey. Selena has gathered up the money. Not looking at me, she scurries into the cafeteria. The other kids start trickling in behind her. Mel looks to Tate for instructions. Tate jerks her head and stalks through the crowd, Mel tagging after her.

Hud says, "Funny thing, Sigrid—I wouldn't have pegged you as suicidal."

He's not what you'd call smiling. But at least he's talking to me. "I'm clean crazy, taking on Tate," I say. "I know what she's like. From the inside, I guess you could say."

"I guess you could."

He saunters into the cafeteria, I follow him, stand at the end of the line, and sit by myself with my back to the wall. Hud's sitting alone on the other side of the room. Prinny is with Travis, Laice, Hector, Cole, and Buck. When Travis says something, they all laugh, even Hector who's so tongue-tied you scarcely know he has a tongue.

I sure blew any plans I might have had for rejoining the Shrikes.

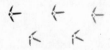

Mr. Murphy watches me to the front door. I have the house to myself. I lock both doors and all the windows even though it's a half-decent day and some fresh air would be good.

Fresh air...I don't ever want to be a Shrike again.

I change into my old duds, haul out the vacuum cleaner and the Windex, and fire the living-room curtains into the garbage.

Too bad, Ma.

If I look back, I think my real dad leaving for Fort McMurray and never coming home even though the company would've paid for the trip—it took my mother by surprise. She'd lost interest in him, sure—Ady's 48" flatscreen with satellite hook-up had become a bigger draw than my dad. But she hadn't expected him to take off. For a few months she stayed home more, cooked the occasional meal, even vacuumed.

Then Seal comes into town, good-looking, good-natured Seal, and lands himself a job at the liquor store. She starts buying wine. She's no drinker. Seal falls for her and who can blame him? He moves in. For over a year, everything's hunky-dory. My mother's happy, and our own TV is turned off soon as Seal walks in the door.

It doesn't last. She goes back to Ady's, first during the days, then evenings, as their eBay business takes off. For a year, there was a lot of yelling—the same kind of yelling I remember before my real dad took off. After that, Seal went quiet. Like he knew he couldn't compete with antique glass and yard sales.

He started hanging out at Tim Hortons when he wasn't working. And now, unless Tate is stringing me a line and I don't think she is, he's dating someone else.

I spray Windex and wipe the glass as though clean windows will solve all my problems.

When Seal comes home after his shift, the room's tore apart. "Another trip to the mall?" he says.

"Can you afford new curtains and a cover for the couch?" Which is my cue to say I know where he spent the night.

"Pay day yesterday," he says, patting the wallet in his back pocket. "Why don't we leave now, and we'll pick up a pizza on the way home? So we don't mess up the kitchen."

"I dunno why I'm doing all this cleaning."

He straightens the hose on the vacuum. "You make any new friends?"

"Not yet."

"Are you cleaning the house because you're afraid of knocking on other kids' doors?"

"Huh?"

"Think about it. Did you measure the windows?"

"I'm cleaning the house because my mother sure isn't going to."

He winces. We leave for town.

He has an errand at Home Hardware, so I start searching for slipcovers and curtains in the mall across the way. I'm rushing from one store to the next when I nearly bump into a woman who's scooting out of the religious bookstore. "Sorry!" I gasp.

It's Mrs. Cody, Tate's mother, Mr. Cody on her heels. Her dress is beige and shapeless, peppered with little black squiggles like worms; he's in a black suit, same as the undertaker's at the funeral parlor. When they recognize me, their faces harden.

Mr. Cody says, "The Lord sits in judgment on sinners."

Mrs. Cody says, "They shall be cast into everlasting flames."

Which of them cut Tate's hair, hacking at it with scissors, the blades flashing in the light?

I scuttle around them and run back to Home Hardware. I need Seal, easy-going Seal with his friendly blue eyes.

He's at the checkout, chatting with the young guy who's passing him the VISA slip. What if my mother had glommed onto someone like Mr. Cody? And wouldn't I rather have Lissie Sugden as my mother than Mrs. Cody?

Seal sees me and waves his bottle of windshield washer at me, smiling. I march up to him, my feelings tumbling around like clothes in the dryer, and blurt, "I love you."

My face turns red. So does his. All these years and have I ever told him how I feel about him? At first, I missed my real dad too much; then before you know it, Seal and my mother were at odds; and once I turned twelve, it seemed kind of childish.

Right there in Home Hardware, other shoppers brushing past us, he puts his arms around me in a clumsy hug. "I love you, too."

I really do love him. It isn't blackmail, so he'll keep living at home. At least, I hope it isn't.

We find what we're looking for and drive home. After we eat the pizza, we fit the dark brown slipcover on the couch, and I arrange the new cushions, turquoise, white and brown, two on one side, one on the other. Then we hang the curtains that match the cushions. The floor's already vacuumed and wet-mopped, lemon oil on the old coffee table, and ever since we left Home Hardware, I've been nerving myself to ask him about Davina.

Can't do it. I'm too scared of the answer. What if he moves out?

I also bought a new floor mat, which I put at the front

door with a big note on top. LORNE SUGDEN—BOOTS OFF!!

Which is when I realize the real reason I'm cleaning the house. It's to keep Lorne and Seal home, the both of them. To make it so nice, they won't leave me.

FOURTEEN

to ruin

If I thought that taking on Mel and Tate near the cafeteria would make kids flock to me desperate to be my best buddy, I was wrong.

We're kept in at recess and noon because it's raining, a steady drizzle that can soak through your jacket in no time. Mel stays on the bus in Long Bight, then stands up with Tate for the first stop in Fiddlers Cove. Hud's gazing out the window, while Prinny and Laice are chattering away like me and Hanna used to.

Mr. Murphy smiles at me. "Take care," he says.

I run for the house. Tate and Mel are strolling toward her place like Mr. and Mrs. Cody have given them their blessing. Indoors, I go through the usual routine. It's mid-June. Even though it's drizzling, I don't want to close every window in the house. But I do it anyway.

I flip on the radio. Old-fashioned disco, the kind of beat Hanna and me used to dance to, and suddenly I miss her so sharp it's like she left yesterday. Flinging the refrigerator door open, I decide to fix myself a snack. More for comfort than because I'm hungry. If only it was

January, so I wouldn't mind being under house arrest.

I reach for the Cheez Whiz.

"You gonna share that, Sigrid?"

The jar drops to the floor, bounces, and rolls. Very slowly, I turn around.

Tate is leaning against the table. Mel's standing by the door. I say faintly, "I locked both doors. How did you get in?"

Tate sneers at me. "Wouldn't you like to know?"

The motor on the fridge starts to whir. I close the door, turn the radio off, and stoop to pick up the jar of Cheez Whiz, my brain scuttling in tight little circles. "Want a snack?" I say.

My phone's on my bureau. Not a hope of getting past Mel.

Tate looks around. "Who cleaned the place up? It wasn't Seal, he's hardly ever home. Can't imagine it was Lorne. Must've been you, right?"

She wanders closer to the sink, fingers the crisp hem of the new curtains. "I hear Davina keeps a clean house. Good cook, too. Are you a good cook, Sigrid?"

I once saw Buck's cat play with a bird, the bird paralysed with fear, the cat lifting its claws then pouncing again just as the wings started to flutter. Wings that were wet with cat spit. Our landline phone's on the table. Might as well be on Knucklebones.

"Seal works until ten tonight," Tate says, "and Lorne's

on late shift at the garage. So we're on our own, just the three of us. Cosy, eh?"

Mel shifts impatiently. "Let's get on with it."

"No hurry," Tate says. "On our way in, I noticed new curtains and cushions in the living room. Is Seal feeling guilty? Is that why he's forking out the dough?"

"You'd have to ask him," I say. *Truculent* was how Mr. Marsden described the Emperor Napoleon, and truculent is how I make myself sound, even though inside I'm as terrified as Prinny the afternoon we cornered her on the wharf.

Tate opens the flour canister, peers inside, and sifts flour through her fingers. Very deliberately, she sprinkles some on the floor.

I take a step forward. "Don't!"

Tate takes a bigger handful. "How about I spell your name?" She starts spilling a steady stream on the linoleum. "S – I – G – R – "

"You're getting it on your sneakers."

"You let me worry about that," Tate says, picks up the canister, and dumps the rest of the flour on the counter.

As a big white cloud settles on the toaster, the coffeemaker, and the sink tray, I lunge at her. "Stop it!"

Mel grabs me from behind, pinning my elbows to my sides. I throw myself forward, breathing in flour, so angry I forget to be afraid. "Tate, so help me, if you mess up my kitchen, I'll sic Seal on you."

"I don't think that would be a good idea," Tate says. "Not unless you want your mother to see this photo my cousin took."

She holds it out. Seal is standing beside a small blue car, his arm around a woman wearing a plain green dress; he's smiling into her eyes as if no one else in the world exists.

It's Davina Murphy.

"My mother already knows about him and Davina." I sound convincing, even to myself.

"I don't think so—your mother's too busy buying and selling to have time for gossip."

Smiling, Tate wanders into the pantry. "Oh my," she says, "everything in prissy little rows."

With one sweep of her arm, she topples ketchup, pickles, jam, and peanut butter onto the floor. The jar of jam cracks open, strawberries seeping onto the green swirls on the linoleum.

I bash my heel into Mel's shin, hitting bone through my sneaker. Elbow her in the gut, pull free, and shove Tate hard. Her elbow cracks against a shelf. She screeches, "Get her, Mel!"

Mel's big body fills the door to the pantry.

Stupid, stupid, why didn't I run for the living room while I had the chance?

Slowly she advances on me, her eyes bright with anticipation. Terror knifes through the rage in my chest.

"This time," Tate says, "don't let go of her."

Mel's fingers close on my arm. Her nails dig in, me paralysed like the bird. She yanks me around so I'm facing Tate, snaps her big fist around my other arm. Tate bends over, scoops up some jam, and smears it into my hair. The rest she smears on the wall. Then she opens a container of mustard and trails yellow sauce over the cans of fruit.

"Seal will know who did this," I croak.

"Then you better clean it up before he arrives home. Think of the photo."

She knocks some more stuff on the floor. A can of coffee gets her attention. She picks it up, thoughtfully. "Back up, Mel," she says. "Let's redecorate the living room."

Mel hauls me into the living room, me kicking and throwing myself around as hard as I can because I love what I did to our place and it's killing me to see how easy Tate's wrecking it. "I'll get you for this—both of you. I dunno how or when, but believe me, you'll be sorry."

Tate pries the lid off the can of coffee and sprinkles coffee grains over the couch. Then she brings in the sugar canister and a bottle of the powdered milk Seal prefers to real cream, don't ask me why.

"Better than Tim Hortons," she says, pouring sugar and white powder over the coffee. "Oh look, triple-triple."

In the bathroom she squirts Lorne's shaving cream on

the mirror. *Tate was here.* She pours liquid soap into the toilet and flushes so bubbles overflow down the sides. Then she dumps toilet bowl cleaner into the tub, wafts the counter with hair spray, picks up the red soap dish, looks at it, head to one side, and smashes it on the floor.

The soap dish was the last red one in the store—I knew I had to have it the moment I saw it. I fling my weight backward, driving Mel into the counter. She grunts. My left arm's free, but before I can free the other, she cups her big arm around my throat, half-lifting me off the floor.

"Hold her still, Mel," Tate orders.

I'm not holding still for anyone. I buck and kick. Mel's other arm snakes around my waist. I throw a leftie punch at Tate who says, her own fury rising to meet mine, "Mel, why d'you think I put up with you? Do your job!"

There's a fierce fast tussle, which I lose. Mel's fists clamp my elbows so tight I know I'll have bruises. Calm as if she's at the beauty parlor, Tate takes out my nail polish and paints *traitor* on my arm, her face so close I can see the beginnings of a zit on her chin.

Nail polish stinks. "I'm no traitor, Tate Cody—I saved your skin. Yours and Mel's. I'm gonna write a letter to your father, telling him what you did today."

She doesn't even bat her lashes, which are long and dark, much longer than mine. "Little tug there, Mel."

Mel tugs. Even though I try not to groan, the sound escapes anyway.

"Lots more where that come from," Tate says. "Seal with his arm around Davina...how romantic is that?"

"Were you born mean?" I whisper.

"Let's check out your bedroom," Tate says. "What, no new curtains in here, Sigrid? Don't figure you're worth it?"

My jaw drops. Is that why I didn't ask Seal for money for the matching bedspread and curtains I saw at the mall? Clear as if they're in front of me, I can see the swirls of green and purple, like the colors were dancing.

The bedspread and curtains are still in the store in their plastic wrap. Safe.

Tate tosses stuff out of my drawers onto the floor, rips the bedclothes apart, and smashes the lightbulb from my lamp. Last thing she does is tear the notes from my binders, crushing the paper in her fists. But she knows, and so do I, that it's too late in the year for this to matter very much. Instead of making me feel hopeful—*she's done, she and Mel will leave now*—it only makes me more afraid.

"Kitchen," she says briskly.

Standing by the counter, she stirs macaroni, Graham cracker crumbs, and caramel pudding into the flour already on the floor. How am I gonna clean up all this mess? It'll take hours.

Casually she daubs some of the mix on the window, then stands back. "Maybe I should've been an artist." Without changing her tone, she adds, "Sigrid, never interfere with me and Mel again. At school, on the bus, or on the street. Do you understand?"

Smarten up, Sigrid. Say yes. "Depends what you're up to."

"Guess you don't understand. Mel..."

Mel tips me onto the floor, face first into macaroni and caramel pudding. Then she sits on me, squishing the air from my lungs. Caramel on her fingernails.

"Now do you understand?" Tate says.

"You break my ribs, even my mother will notice."

Mel pushes my face into the floor. I can't breathe. I start to panic, drumming my toes on the floor. Dead weight. Can't budge.

Tate says, "Ease off a little, Mel. Maybe she has something to say."

I can feel Mel's reluctance. But she moves her hand off the back of my neck. I heave in air. "Yeah, I understand."

"You're sure now?"

"I'm sure."

And don't I despise myself for giving in.

"Good," Tate says. "Time for us to leave, Mel, so Sigrid has lots of time to clean up before her men waltz in the door. Leaving their boots on the mat like well-trained puppies."

Mel lurches to her feet. I lie still, hearing their footsteps crunch over the coffee grains and sugar on the living-room floor. The door opens and closes. My cheek falls to the floor. Caramel slimes my ear. Caramel and tears.

Slow tears, dripping on the linoleum, one by one.

FIFTEEN

to lie

A sob works its way past the tightness in my throat. Another one follows. I never cry because what's the point but I'm crying now, crying like Selena and Vi when we bullied them and how's that for justice and I want to go to sleep and wake up tomorrow in my clean and tidy bedroom.

Not a chance.

I cry some more.

Then, moving slow as Danny Grimsby with a hangover, I stagger to my feet. Kleenex to blow my nose. Cold water to scrub at my face and ears until the lumpy caramel mix sluices down the sink. Warm water to wet my hair and rinse the jam out. New towel to dry my face and hair.

Pick the macaroni out of the sink. Breathe deep. Look around.

Almost, I start to cry again.

I should lock the front door.

And that's when I remember that I left my pencil case, with my house key inside, in my desk at recess while I went to the washroom. No trouble for Tate to steal the key, make a copy at noon, then sneak the key back while I was still in the cafeteria.

So *that's* how they got in.

If Tate has a key, we'll have to change the locks. If I tell Seal what happened, Tate will give that photo to my mother.

I'll lie to him.

All evening to concoct one simple lie. And clean up the mess.

I start in my bedroom, because that's easiest fixed. I have enough money in my bank account to buy that snazzy bedspread and curtains. I'm gonna do it. I'm worth it, worth every cent, $59.99 plus tax.

So there, Tate Cody.

I gash my finger on the smashed light bulb. Does blood wash off a floor easier than flour, macaroni, and caramel? Stay tuned.

After shaking the cushions on the couch, I plug in the vacuum. I'm some glad Tate didn't touch the curtains, and that the coffee was dry and didn't stain the new cushions.

Bathroom next. I near to lose heart when I see the red shards of the soap dish scattered over the floor. First thing I do is scrub *traitor* off my arm with polish remover, its acetone-smell fighting with the ammonia-smell of the toilet bowl cleanser in the tub. Worst part of the clean-up is the hair spray, sticky on the counter. Vim works, though, along with elbow grease. At least the bath mat's clean, and the towels.

The kitchen takes forever. I go through six buckets of water cleaning the shelves in the pantry, the kitchen counters, and the linoleum. Mustard, flour, jam, macaroni, graham cracker crumbs, ground coffee, sugar, powdered milk, and caramel pudding all get added to the Saturday grocery list.

I pour the last bucket down the sink. It's 10:04. Lorne got off work at nine, so he must be with Sally. Quickly I run to my bedroom to change my clothes, pulling on a long-sleeved shirt in case Mel left marks on my arms.

When Seal comes in the door, shucking off the black shoes with arch support that he wears to work, I'm in the kitchen, making myself a peanut butter and banana sandwich because there isn't any jam. "Hi," I say, natural as can be. "Want something to eat?"

He rubs his chin. He looks tired. "Yeah...tea and raisin toast?"

He disappears into the bathroom. I use Red Rose tea, two bags because he likes it strong, and toast the bread just the way he likes it, not a trace of burnt. He comes back in, wearing a clean t-shirt. "What happened to the soap dish?"

"I broke it. Knocked it to the floor by accident."

"Too bad," he says and eases into the chair.

I pass him the milk. There's something about his blue

eyes—I hate lying to him. "Seal, I found out today that Tate stole my front door key and made a copy of it. Can you buy a new lock tomorrow?"

"She did? Why?"

"Wants to keep me on edge, I guess."

"Stealing our house key—that's a matter for the cops."

"No sense bringing the cops in! A new lock, that's all we need."

He stares at me. "You look wiped. She giving you grief?"

"Nothing I can't handle."

"If she's pushing you around, you tell me, and I'll go straight to the principal."

He doesn't look nearly as tired as he did two minutes ago. I manage—just—to keep my voice steady. "No, it's okay."

"I'm on the late shift again tomorrow," he says, calming down. "So I'll buy the locks in the morning and install them before I go to work. I'll drop your new key off at school."

I have the weird feeling he knows I've been lying to him ever since he walked into the kitchen.

Mel gets off in Long Bight the next afternoon, and Tate marches straight to her place once she's off the bottom step of the bus, dropping her chain link earrings in her pack as she goes. She didn't say a word about the photo of Seal and Davina all day.

Her hair's still a wreck; she's made no attempt to trim the jagged ends, as if she's sticking them in your face and daring you to react. I wore the same long-sleeved shirt to school because I do have bruises. Big ones.

I unlock the door with my new key. House is clean and tidy, although you can still catch a whiff of Pine Sol.

I bet Seal smelled it last night. Along with acetone and ammonia.

It's a decent day, a few dust-bunny clouds hanging in the sky. After checking through the living-room windows that there's no sign of Tate, I wheel my bike out of the garage and race down the road past her place. Blinds drawn, front door shut, lawn with a buzz cut.

I'll go to Gulley Cove. I like it there. Maybe I'll detour to Abe's barn on the way.

As I approach Hud's place, he's walking from their tarpaper shed to the house. No lawn at Hud's, with or without a buzz cut. Dandelions galore, but even their happy faces can't make his house look anything but droop-shouldered.

Doyle Quinn, Hud's dad, slams out the side door. As he strides past Hud, he flashes out a fist and belts Hud on the side of the head.

Hud reels sideways. My front tire hits the shoulder and

the bike veers toward the ditch. I pull it straight, one foot to the ground.

Doyle keeps going, casual as if he swatted a moose fly. Hud's still standing there, his head down.

Are you okay?

Of course he's not.

I start pedaling, praying he doesn't look up and see me. How can a father do that to his son? Hit him. Hit him hard enough to knock him off-balance.

My most vivid memory of my real dad is him pushing me on the swing in the backyard, me squealing in that delicious mixture of fear and delight, him calling, "Higher, Sigrid? Do you want to go higher?"

And I always did.

After he shaved—first thing in the morning—he rubbed stuff on his face that smelled of cinnamon.

He never once lifted a hand to me. As for Seal, I can't imagine him hitting anything.

How *dare* Doyle hit Hud? Hud, who came to my rescue.

Into my mind drop the different times I've seen Hud come to school with bruises and scrapes. I've heard him say to Mr. Murphy, *My snowmobile tipped,* and to Mr. Marsden, *I tripped on the stairs.* The day he rescued me, he told me he'd fallen off his bike.

Lies. All of them lies.

Even if I'd thought of my smartphone, I couldn't have taken a photo of that punch—it happened too fast.

I've reached the edge of the cliffs. Bike in the grass, butt on the rock where Hud was sitting the day I tried to talk to him. The horizon shimmers. The waves aren't putting any muscle into their punches at the rocks.

Doyle's skinny, but he's tall and wiry. He scarce looked at Hud when he belted him, as though hitting his son was a habit he'd gotten into, like grinding his cigarette butts under his heel.

Anger still churning away inside me.

About time somebody did something.

Sixteen

to avenge

I sit there quite a while. Soft slosh of the sea, sunlight sparking the waves. Wild strawberries in bloom, creamy-white. A shiny brown beetle climbs up a blade of grass, falls off the end, climbs up the next one. Sorta like cleaning house. Hasn't taken me long to realize that new curtains don't put an end to dust bunnies.

Voices drift up the hill, and the rattle of stones. Prinny and Laice bicycle over the crest, talking away like there's no tomorrow. They see me.

"Hi," I say.

Laice tilts her pretty little nose. Prinny nods. They pump harder until they're past me.

Up until now, I didn't feel lonesome.

I ride straight home, where—after organizing the stuff I'll need—I try to nap. It doesn't work. So I'm still wide awake when Seal comes home. Lorne's back soon after. Neither one stays up long. Once the lights are off and Lorne's snoring, I climb out of bed and dress in the clothes I laid out on my chair: black tights, black sweater, black socks.

I'm no Shrike. Not any more.

I'm Sigrid the Avenger.

I creep out my door, pad across the living-room floor, pick up my sneaks, and softly unsnib the lock. The new key on a string around my neck.

Keeping to the shoulder of the road, ready to duck into the trees if I hear a truck or a car coming, I walk east. Past Tate's house. Past Our Lady of the Reefs church. There's a light shining on the statue of Mary in her blue robe, the baby sleeping in her arms, her head bent so she won't miss one move he makes.

Past the burned-out shell of the chandler's store, the Herbey place, and Joe Rideout's. A gap in the houses, then Hud's place. The back door light is on, shining on the yard with its tarpaper shed. Doyle's truck is parked in the driveway. The house is in darkness.

I tiptoe to the side of the truck that faces away from the house, kneel down, unzip my pack, and take out the roofing nails I stole from Seal's tool chest. Carefully I sprinkle a few behind the rear tire, making sure the sharp ends are pointing up.

A while ago, Seal told me Doyle takes off for Tim Hortons early every morning for his caffeine fix. I'm hoping at least one of the nails will puncture the tire, giving him a slow leak that will be flat by the time he's drunk his coffee. Then he'll have to change to the spare and fix the flat.

Lousy beginning to his day. And no way he can blame Hud.

Joe Rideout's dog barks. Once. Twice.

I scramble to my feet, edge away from the truck, and sprint down the road, my palms damp, my pulse racing.

Is it breaking the law to puncture someone's tire?

Is it breaking the law to punch your son?

Lights on at Joe's. I slide into the trees, going slow, stumbling over roots and rocks. The dog barks harder, then falls quiet as Joe calls its name. His front door pulls shut.

As I barrel past the church, it seems like Mary's frowning at me. "Avengers don't sit home eating peanut butter sandwiches," I say to her, panting.

No lights on at our house, so no one's missed me. Worst part is unlocking the door and slinking inside, then locking it again. Lorne's still snoring. He's a champion snorer. He'd better not wake Seal.

Even though it's dark, I can pick out the pattern on the new cushions. I'm across the floor and into my room, easing the door shut. Then I'm sitting on the bed, trembling all over. Being an Avenger is hard on the nerves. Imagine being a full-time criminal.

I get undressed, hide my black clothes in the closet, and climb into bed.

I try to settle to sleep. I count imaginary dandelions, flocks of seagulls, piles of tires.

My heart gives an almighty thump. Sitting up straight, staring into the darkness, I remember how Doyle slammed his way out of the house, strode toward Hud, and whacked him for no reason, then kept going as though Hud wasn't made of flesh and blood, as though he was no more important than a stick of furniture.

I've just done something guaranteed to put Doyle Quinn in a bad mood. Doesn't matter that he can't blame Hud for the flat. He'll take it out on him anyway. Of course he will.

Any hope of sleep has gone. I have to sneak back to Doyle's and scrabble in the dirt until I've found every single nail I dropped. But just as I swing my legs over the edge of the bed, a car pulls in our driveway. The front door opens and closes. The TV switches on.

My mother. Home a day early. What if she'd been here when I was sneaking in the door?

She's a light sleeper.

I can't go back to Hud's place now.

No amount of cold water splashed on my face can make it look anything but puffy-eyed. When I walk outside to wait for the bus, Tate is already standing there, the breeze playing with the black clumps of her hair, the usual mess of chains dangling. She gives me the once-over. "You don't look so hot."

"Nice earrings if you're a metalhead. Seal changed the locks on the doors."

"Don't get too big for them Nikes of yours."

The bus pulls up. Good timing. When she uses that quiet voice, it sets my nerves rattling like her chains.

I follow her up the steps. Prinny, Laice, Travis, and Hector are sitting in their usual seats. Hud isn't on the bus.

My nails dig into my palms. "Where's Hud, Mr. Murphy?"

"His mother said he was sick. Sit down, Sigrid, I'm running late."

Sick...

It's sports day. No one wants me on their team even though I can run fast. I'll never be forgiven for being a Shrike.

I win a couple of events because all the way around the track I can feel Hud on my heels, Hud with his scraped face and bruised jaw.

Hud, who isn't in school today.

On Saturday morning, I go into town with Seal. Wincing, I notice Doyle's truck parked outside the tavern. Seal says casually, "Doyle Quinn had a flat yesterday morning...I stopped to give him a hand. Sour-faced guy, barely bothered to thank me."

My stomach clenches. I stare out the window.

Once we're at the mall, I show him the bedspread and curtains, with their purple and green swirls. They're reduced to $49.95. "You wouldn't rather have the ones with the pink roses?" he says dubiously.

"I like these. If you put them on your card, I'll go to the machine and pay you back."

We both know this means my real dad will be buying me the new bedspread. "Okay," he says, and I can't read his face.

While he's at the barber's, I run up the street to the animal shelter. The receptionist, who has a ginger kitten draped over her shoulder, says, "Fifty dollars? That's very generous of you—we need cat food and litter, so it'll be put to good use."

The kitten reminds me of Prinny's ginger cat, purring in my arms.

She pats the kitten, writes me a receipt, smiles at me like she means it, and I walk out. Making amends doesn't always leave you feeling good; I thought when I finally got rid of the fifty bucks, I'd be dancing on the street.

How can I dance on the street when I feel so guilty about Prinny's cats?

How can I dance anywhere when I don't know what's happened to Hud?

At the mall, in an effort to cheer myself up, I buy a classy blue shirt with long sleeves. Then I run to the bank machine, meet Seal at FoodMart, and pay him cash for the bedspread and curtains.

Back home, I take them out of the plastic package; Seal helps me hang the curtains. When my dad sends this month's fifty dollars, I might buy a poster for the wall.

Will a poster cheer me up any more than the shirt or the curtains?

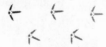

Keeping an eye out for Tate, I bike up the road. No sign of Hud, not around his place, near the cliffs, or at Gulley Cove. Doyle's truck is still gone when I get back. Trying to act like I just caught sight of something valuable in the driveway, I scrabble around in the dirt and find two of the nails. Quickly I pocket them, then race home.

It's like Hud's vanished off the face of the earth.

Seal stays out late both nights on the weekend. Avoiding my mother, I figure.

Monday morning, second last day of school, is also report card day. We have to take them home to be signed, then bring them back Tuesday morning so Mrs. Dooks can check them off. Once that's done, they release us for the summer.

I wear my new blue shirt over a white tank top, with a dusting of blue eye shadow and a flick of mascara for courage.

Hud is on the bus, sitting near the back like usual. When I near to faint with relief, I realize way down I was terrified that he was dead. Crazy, I know, major crazy, but fears are fears because they grasp you by the throat, not by the brain cells.

He's wearing shades, and a long-sleeved sweatshirt even though it's warm. Why would he do that unless it's to hide bruises, like I've had to hide mine?

Once we get to school, he disappears into his classroom.

Mrs. Dooks has given up trying to teach us anything, so she reads to us all morning. At recess, I run to the washroom. While I'm washing my hands, Mel clomps in, her hair hanging straight and greasy on either side of her face.

"Thought I saw you come in here," she says.

Nicole Greene waltzes into the washroom. "Out,"

Mel says. Nicole smirks at me and leaves without a backward look.

Mel says, "Won't be seeing much of you after school's out, Sigrid."

"I'll buy Kleenex."

Mel's brow furrows.

"To mop up my tears," I say.

"Smart-ass!"

I remember how she made me say stuff I didn't want to say by wiping my face in caramel sauce on the kitchen floor. "I won't miss your ugly mug, not for one minute."

She heads for me, pure *mean* gleaming in her eyes. I fill my palm with pink foam from the soap dispenser and smear it over her mouth so she looks like a rabid pink poodle. No chance to laugh because she's shoving me against the wall. I say, so normal I amaze myself, "Oh, Mrs. Dooks, were you looking for me?"

Mel jerks, her grip loosening as she glances over her shoulder. I pull free and haul on the door. When it's halfway open, she rips my new blue shirt out of my waistband. I twist frantically, leaving the shirt in her hands. That's when I see Hud, standing outside the guys' washroom, staring at me.

"Hi," I say.

Mel sees Hud and gives him an evil look. She drops the shirt on the floor, and before she marches down the corridor, she wipes her feet on it.

She forgot to wipe her mouth.

"You sure attract trouble," Hud says, pushing his shades up into his hair.

There's a nasty scrape on his knuckle. One eye is swollen almost shut, the bruises like a rainbow if you leave out green and orange.

A sick lump slithers, ice-cold, down my throat to my gut. I whisper, "What happened?"

"Walked into a door."

"No, you didn't."

"You could be right."

"Your dad did it."

"Nah," he drawls, "what would he do that for?"

Nails on a dirt driveway..."Because he was in a bad mood?"

"He's never in a good mood."

"A while ago, I saw him hit you."

Something lethal chills Hud's eyes. "You oughta cool that imagination of yours, Sigrid."

"You oughta ice that eye of yours, Hud."

Lethal vanishes, replaced by—yeah, it's laughter. Then it vanishes, too. He turns on his heel and walks away. He's doing his best to hide a limp.

I should've confessed. Told him straight out that I put nails behind his dad's tire, so I'm to blame for his multi-colored eye and his sore leg. And what about his scraped knuckle? Did he fight back?

Where was his mother? He has a little sister, too, who you hardly ever see.

The scrambled eggs I had for breakfast curdle in my stomach.

My career as an Avenger is over. I did less damage as a Shrike.

Seventeen

to spy

Seal comes home at six and so does Lorne. Lorne's still dating Sally Parsons, and looks like he's not getting enough sleep. Doesn't hurt his appetite for supper, which is lasagna with Caesar salad. At least in the kitchen I don't do any damage.

We got our report cards that afternoon. After we eat, Seal gives mine his full attention. "You did good, Sigrid," he says, and signs on the dotted line.

Neither of us suggests getting my mother to sign on the other dotted line.

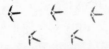

The last day of school is mercifully short—just an hour in the morning. Mr. MacInney gives his usual pep talk over the intercom. *Have a safe summer, respect your parents, and don't litter.*

So I won't litter.

Mrs. Dooks goes through our report cards, checks each of us off on her list, tells us not to forget to read our assigned novel over the summer, and smiles in relief as we troop out the door. I'm going down the front steps wondering if I'll have the chance to talk to Hud when a foot comes from nowhere and I'm on my knees on the pavement, hitting so hard I give a choked cry.

Tate says, "Oops...sorry."

There's a rip in the knee of my jeans.

I push myself up, shame just as bad as the pain in my knees because kids are staring at me. Joan Bidson snickers. Prinny looks uncomfortable. Laice is frowning.

Travis says, "Tate, lay off! Just because Sigrid had the guts to quit your group, you don't have to pick on her."

"I'll do what I want," Tate says.

Ain't that the truth.

I shuffle toward the bus. Like Hud, I'm trying not to limp.

Climbing the steps hurts bad. Travis is already sitting down next to Laice. Eyes glued to the black mat that goes from front to back, I mumble, "Thanks, Travis."

Mel gets off in Long Bight. Tate waits for me to hobble down the steps. "See you around," she says, same words everyone's saying, but hers are a threat.

I let myself in the house. In the kitchen, there's a note on the table and a card propped against the salt shaker. I read the note first. Seal has to work a double shift today because two guys called in sick; but Lorne will be home for supper. The card says, *Congratulations!* in purple letters over a whirlpool of colors. Not a rose in sight. Tears prick my eyes. Seal loves me enough to choose a card he knows I'll like rather than one he likes.

My real dad loved me...*higher, higher*...and he left anyway.

I find an old pair of jeans, throw the torn ones in the hamper, and daub antibiotic cream on my knees. After making myself a snack of Cheez Whiz and crackers, I walk out on the back deck. The mosquitoes are wicked. I go back inside. I eat the snack. I don't turn the TV on. I pick up our assigned novel and put it down again. I was so busy looking forward to no school for two months that I forgot I don't have anyone to hang with.

What am I going to do all summer?

I vacuum the floors in all the rooms except Lorne's. I wipe the counters in the kitchen and bathroom. Seal already did the breakfast dishes. I'm finished and it's only noon. I make lunch even though I'm not hungry. I wash and rinse my plate and glass. It's 12:27.

I put a load through the washer and hang it on the line. 1:13.

I ride to St. Fabien, lock my bike to the rack outside the mall, and check out posters in a couple of stores. I don't want graceful ballet dancers in frilly skirts, or cute little kittens that remind me of Prinny's cats. I don't want a sailboat tipped sideways on the waves like it has someplace real important to go and it's getting there fast.

I bicycle home. In the cookbook there's a recipe for chicken breasts baked in mushroom soup and parmesan cheese. I'll make that for me and Lorne. I even boil rice, along with carrots and turnip.

It's ready at five-thirty. Lorne's not home. I call the garage where he works. He left half an hour ago. I call him on his cell and get voice mail. "Lorne, supper's ready," I say and push End. I text him with the same message.

No reply.

My own brother couldn't even come home on the last day of school.

The chicken's getting cold. I sit down at the table and chew my way through meat, rice, and veggies, listening to myself swallow, forcing food past the panic.

Two months and two weeks before school starts again. All those days, and what will I fill them with? Who will I talk to?

Hud sometimes speaks to me, but he'll quit if I tell him about the tire.

Travis stuck up for me on the school steps, but he'd stick up for anyone if he thought wrong was being done.

Prinny looks at me like I'm a bad smell and Laice is too classy for the likes of me. Hector will grunt at me same as he grunts at most people. You can't live on a diet of grunts.

I remember how lonely I was two years ago when Hanna left. That was the summer I hooked up with Tate and Mel, and right now I understand why.

I wash the dishes, put them away, and listen to the silence. I open Lorne's door and look from the unmade bed to the greasy pizza box that's bottom-up on the floor. I'm not gonna wash *his* sheets or clean his room. Why couldn't he have come home for once?

I think about Mel, cornering me in the girls' washroom, and Tate, tripping me in front of the whole school. Instead of lying around feeling sorry for myself, wimpy as Vi Dunston, why don't I do something about all this?

Sigrid the Avenger hasn't retired. Maybe she blew her first assignment, but she won't blow the second one, or the third.

Because she'll do her research.

I march right out to the garage and bike to Long Bight. Long Bight draws the tourists in droves, because of its old saltbox houses perched on granite, its weathered fish stages, and shrimp boats. Terns chirr overhead. Gulls shriek into the wind. Cameras click from June to October.

Mel's place is tucked off by itself above a little cove. Lilies are growing tall against the front wall, a couple of orange flowers already out; pink and white roses are opening by the shed. The lawn needs a good mow. No truck in the driveway.

I bet Mel's mother planted the flowers.

I hide my bike in the shrubbery and creep down the slope, coming at the house from behind the shed. After I sneak across the gap, I peer in one of the back windows. It's the living room. Looks like it's never used.

I crawl to the next window and edge my head up so I can just see through the screen. My pulse jolts. Mel's bedroom. Nothing fancy in it except an antique dresser with a mirror in a carved frame, and a poster on the far wall of Carly Rae Jepsen in a big, orange hat and a slinky top.

The room's empty.

Through the open window I hear dishes clattering, then a tap running—Mel's in the kitchen. I slump below the sill.

The microwave beeps, then silence. Clump of footsteps, closer and closer. A door bangs shut. I wait a few seconds before I inch upright, poised to run like a rabbit if Mel catches sight of me.

On the bed is a plate with three hot dogs slathered in ketchup and relish. Mel's standing beside the poster. With her pudgy finger she's tracing Carly's shiny dark hair, deep blue eyes, flushed cheeks, and high cheekbones.

Then Mel leans over the dresser and stares at her reflection, into pale, pink-rimmed eyes set too close together. With the same finger, she traces her cheek—

not a cheekbone in sight, just a zit near the corner of her mouth. With the other hand she tugs some greasy strands of hair behind her ear and turns her head this way and that, stretching her neck as if she's trying to get rid of her double chin.

Her head droops. She shuts her eyes. I watch, fascinated, horrified, as a tear slides down the bulge of her cheek and drips onto her XXL t-shirt.

I sink downward, hands flat to the shingles. If she sees me, she'll kill me.

Ducking behind the shed, I scramble up the slope and haul my bike out of the shrubs. Leaves are caught in the spokes. In granny gear, I pump up the last of the hill, then I'm off, racing toward home as though Mel really is chasing me.

I never knew she cared how she looks. Or that she wanted to be different.

Mind you, it's none too smart comparing yourself to the likes of Carly Rae, not unless you're drop-dead gorgeous like Laice Hadden and how many of us are that lucky?

Smart never was Mel's strong suit.

Now what does the Avenger do?

Revenge and retaliation don't seem to be on the list.

Back home, I curl up on my new bedspread in my PJs and read a book about a bunch of high-school girls who do nothing but bicker about clothes and boys. For a break, I Google Carly Rae on my smartphone; her eyes are truly beautiful, and I could learn a thing or two from her about make-up.

When Seal comes home at ten-thirty, I thank him for the card and try not to show how pathetically grateful I am to talk to another human being. Afterward, I go to bed.

Mel's face, so hopeless, so baffled...I was planning on spying on Tate the same way, but now I'm not so sure. Being an Avenger is complicated.

Eighteen

to apologize

Next day is the first full day of no school. Late last night, I heard my mother's car pull in, heard her and Seal arguing in the living room. He slept on the couch again. She was gone by seven this morning.

She uses our place as a motel, that's how I see it.

Seal tells me before he leaves for work that he won't be back for supper, but that Lorne's promised to be home all evening.

"Yeah?" I say.

"What are you planning to do today?"

"Haven't decided yet."

"There must be kids around here you can do stuff with," he says, sounding impatient, like I'm a problem waiting to be fixed.

I shrug. "If there are, I'll find them."

"Have a good one," he says, pats me like I'm a stray dog, and pushes his feet into his black shoes.

I shower, wash my hair, and blow it dry, moving slow. The slower I move, the slower the clock moves. Then I pack sandwiches and take off for Gulley Cove. Doyle's truck is parked in the yard, not a glimpse of Hud. I'm approaching Abe's place when Abe comes out his side door, his dog Lucy on his heels.

After leaning my bike against his fence, I push the gate open. Barking, Lucy gallops toward me. When I hold out my hand, she licks it, so I tell her she's a good dog. Lifting his old ball cap to scratch his head, Abe watches me walk up the path.

I take a deep breath. "I'm Sigrid Sugden, Mr. Murphy, and I don't have any friends because I used to be a bully so I've got a bad rep. But I'm doing my best to change and can I sit in your barn sometimes in the hopes the white cat will come down from the loft and keep me company?"

He slaps at a mosquito with his cap. Even though he's gnarled-up, his movements are jerky as a squirrel's. "I don't got much truck with change, meself," he says. "Though I do have to say Travis Keating has a way of pushin' me into doin' stuff I wasn't cogitatin' on doin'. Here's me with two cats in the house scarce stirrin' off the couch, another in the barn, and me buyin' prime cat food."

"If I don't change, no one will ever speak to me."

"How d'you know a cat lives in the loft?"

"I went into your barn one day when you weren't here."

"Did you now? And what if the cat does come down?

You gonna throw rocks at it same way Hud Quinn throws rocks at my dog?"

"He *does?*"

"I seen him with me own eyes."

"Hud's not as bad as you might think. He—"

"Tell that to Lucy," Abe says. "If he's a buddy o' yours, I'm not so sure about lettin' you in the barn."

"I promise I won't harm the cat! Any of your cats. Or the dog."

"Promises are cheap as blackflies in June."

I say desperately, "The streak of mean in me—I want it gone."

"We all got mean in us, girl, and you're skittery as that white cat...you won't bother me hens none? Not high on brains, hens, but I has a fondness for 'em."

"I won't. Truly I won't."

He rubs his hand over the stubble on his chin, his faded blue eyes crafty. "What's in this for me?"

"I could do some chores for you."

"You'd look right good shovelin' manure."

I gulp. "Okay."

"Prinny and Travis know about this?"

I shake my head. "Prinny doesn't like me. I don't know how Travis feels."

He cackles. "You'll sort it, when all three o' you turns up at once. C'mon in the barn and I'll show you where I keeps the shovel and the cat treats."

I didn't realize I'd been holding my breath until it escapes in a small *whoosh*. I follow him through the old wooden door into the barn.

The pig rustles in his fresh straw. The hens scratch in the feed. Ghost, the white cat, eyes us from the rafters as Abe shows me where the cow is tied at night. "Manure pile is out back—use the wheelbarrow in the corner. Then spread a little fresh straw from them bales."

The plastic bottle of treats is on a shelf near the door. "Not too many," he says. "Regular food's in that bucket. You be after puttin' the lid on tight. Cold water tap's over there—don't leave it drippin'. And make sure you latches the barn door tight shut."

He tosses some pellets into the pig's trough. "Goin' to town. You be okay?"

"Thank you, Mr. Murphy."

"Abe's me name, girl. And I'm trustin' you."

"You can," I say fervently, and watch him leave.

Ghost throws back his head. *Eeeeeooowww...*

For the first time in three days, I'm smiling. The pig's table manners aren't the best. As the hens strut in and out, Ghost starts to wash himself. I lean back against the straw, watching him. I wouldn't hurt him for the world.

Wishing Hud hadn't thrown rocks at Lucy, wishing I'd told Abe about Doyle Quinn, I doze off...

Straw is prickling the back of my neck. Then the rooster crows outside and my eyes jerk open. Ghost is crouched over his food bowl, his table manners on a par with the pig's. I don't move a muscle.

My neck's aching by the time he lifts his head, stretches, saunters over to a little hole in the wall, and slips outside. I'm smiling again. Lorne will be home for supper and now I've got myself a summer project. Would Seal let Ghost move in with me?

The old wooden latch on the outside of the barn door is stiff. I wrestle with it because Abe's trusting me to do everything right. When the door's proper shut, I turn around.

Prinny Murphy is striding up the path. She yells, "What are you doing here?"

She plants herself in front of me. She's taller than me.

I say, "I fell asleep in the barn."

"What were you doing in the barn? You're trespassing!"

"Abe told me I could go in."

"And the milk from his cow makes green cheese."

"He did tell me! He trusted me, he said so. Too bad you wouldn't do the same."

"Me? *Trust* you? After what you and the other Shrikes did to my cats? I found Tansy under the shed, no problem, but Rogue was lost overnight and into the next day, me searching for him that night in the rain and the wind. Just lucky I found him, way out on the barrens, before a fox got him. I love my cats—why would I ever trust you?"

"I'm sorry, Prinny...real sorry."

"Like that fixes it?"

"I *am* sorry. I'm doing my best to change my ways—but no one will listen!"

"I can see you're trying," she says grudgingly. "But you were a Shrike for two years—two *years*, Sigrid—and I'm not ready to trust you."

"Then you're just as mean as me." I push past her on the narrow path. "Ghost went outside."

The path is blurry because I'm near to crying. It was so peaceful in the barn. But now whenever I come here, I'll be worrying that Prinny will show up. Her and her friends, too-good-to-be-true Travis Keating and beautiful, stuck-up Laice Hadden.

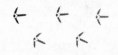

I heat up leftover chicken for supper with fresh veggies. Lorne doesn't come home. I don't bother phoning or texting him. What's the use?

I wash the dishes.

I don't want to ride my bike. I don't want to read about those silly high-school girls. I don't want to vacuum or dust or tidy.

Mel sits heavy on me, like I'm flat on the kitchen floor with her on my back. Hud sits even heavier.

I'm that desperate, I almost wish my mother would walk in the door.

I wake to darkness, my heart bouncing in my chest and all I can see is Mel's eyes, her lashes light as the pig's, as she walks slowly toward me on Knucklebones.

The rest of the dream, gone.

The wind billows my curtains because I forgot to close the window. The venetian blind snicks the glass. I lie still, and slowly the feeling creeps over me, then hardens into certainty. I'm alone in the house.

After a while, I climb out of bed. Lorne's door is wide open, Seal's partway, both beds empty. Lorne's souped-up Honda, Seal's truck, my mother's Camaro—none of them parked in the driveway.

Up until tonight, it's been my mother gone, and occasionally Lorne. Sooner or later, I suppose, it had to happen that all three didn't come home. My mother on a buying trip. Lorne at Sally's. And Seal—I try to ignore the stab of fear—Seal at Davina's?

If he'd had an accident, I'd have heard.

Back in bed, I crawl under the covers. My feet are cold and sleep's like the fog—I can't take ahold of it. Lost is how I feel, lost as a cat on the barrens in a nor'easter.

After a while, I get up again, mix some instant oatmeal

in the kitchen, and eat it at the table, sitting in the dark, listening to the distant sigh of waves on the rocks.

Little by little, the sky starts to lighten. Blackness slides off the spruce trees until they're dark green, full of shadows. The brightest stars are stubborn, as if they don't want to be invisible.

At 4:55, Seal's truck pulls into the driveway. I go to the window. For several long minutes, he just sits there behind the wheel, me watching him, him not knowing I'm watching him. Then he climbs out, shuts the door real quiet, and walks toward the house.

Click of his key in the lock. He shuts the front door the same way, so quiet I'd never have woken. As he walks into the living room, I'm standing at the kitchen door in my pale blue pajamas. He gives a strangled snort.

"Sigrid? You scared me out of a month of Sundays."

"Who else would it be? Seeing as I'm the only one home."

He winces. "I saw Lorne's car was gone."

"He didn't come home for supper, either."

Seal's shoulders slump. "Your mother told me she'd be home last night."

"She comes and goes as she pleases, we all know that."

He's wearing a new short-sleeved shirt, one I've never seen before. "You smell of perfume," I say.

In the pale light I watch a tide of red rise from the neck of his shirt, up his cheeks all the way to his forehead.

"Sorry I'm so late," he mutters, as though I'm the parent and he's the kid.

He walks past me. It's a nice perfume, flowery but not heavy-duty, like the freesias they sell for $7.99 at FoodMart. He goes into his bedroom—his and my mother's bedroom, even though she's scarcely ever in it—and closes the door.

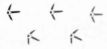

I go back to bed and fall into a dead sleep. I wake up with a headache. Someone's rapping on the front door.

"Coming!"

Bathrobe, tie it up, stumble across the living room. Hair's a mess and mouth tastes like dead fur. The clock says noon. *Noon?*

So much for going to Abe's barn this morning.

Tate Cody is standing on the doorstep. I snap awake. "What d'you want?"

"Good morning to you, too," she says. "Thought you might want to know that your stepdad spent the night at Davina's ."

"I know he did," I say. Fingers twitching in the folds of my blue robe.

"His truck was still parked in her driveway at four o'clock this morning."

"Tate, I hope you know how lucky you are to have two

God-fearing parents who'll never stray one step to the left or the right, and who'll stay married for all eternity."

Her fingers don't just twitch. They curl into fists, waves of hate pouring out of her strong enough to vaporize you. "I'm not done with you," she says.

"Good. Because I'm not done with you, either." I slam the door in her face and flip the lock. The funny thing is, it's true.

Just don't ask me what it means.

NINETEEN

to dictate

I brush my teeth and my hair. I'm getting out of here. I need to spend some serious money on me. Because who the heck else cares about me?

This mood stays with me all the way to St. Fabien. Clouds have rolled in and likely it's gonna rain and I don't care. The poster shop is busy, which gives me lots of time to look around. In the end, I buy two posters. The first one has two sleek cats sitting in the sun on a window sill; one of the cats is white, and reminds me of Ghost. In the other poster, a girl is appearing out of the mist, wearing a long, flowing dress and carrying a sword. A beautiful girl, whose face says, *Don't mess with me*.

The woman at the counter wraps them up. I walk to the liquor store, parading in as though I own the place. The guy at the cash says, "Hi there, Sigrid."

"Is Seal available?"

"I'll fetch him."

"Thank you," I say and go back outside.

Seal hurries through the glass doors. "You okay, Sigrid?"

I still have a headache, but I'm not telling him that. I pass him the package. "Will you put these in your truck and bring them home with you? If you're coming home, that is."

"Now, Sigrid, of course I'm coming home."

"For supper?"

"We have to talk," he says.

"So are you coming home for supper?"

"Right after my shift. Why don't I bring take-out from Pizza Delight?"

"I'm cooking."

"We have to talk," he repeats, stubborn as those early-morning stars.

"I'll listen and I'm cooking."

I walk away. I didn't smile at him once, and the whole time we were talking I felt like that beautiful girl, flashing her sword, cutting the air to shreds. Am I so angry because Seal's still living in my mother's house and he's cheating on her and I thought better of him?

I didn't think I loved my mother enough to care.

Or am I jealous because he's found someone else to love and my life feels like I'm stumbling through the fog with nothing but a kitchen knife in my hand?

Seal's gonna move out...

I push that thought all the way down to the soles of my sneakers and march to the drugstore. I need some new blue eye shadow.

Racks and racks of make-up and that's when I have this totally brilliant idea.

I frown at the racks. Okay, a week ago I had a brilliant idea that involved roofing nails. *Think, Sigrid. Don't blow it a second time.*

Girls like make-up. Mel's a girl.

Make-up makes a difference. No amount of mascara will turn Mel into Carly Rae, but we have to do the best with what we've got and all journeys begin with a single step, Mrs. Dooks said so.

I'd be doing something nice instead of something mean.

Is that the way to become a real Avenger? I feel a little flicker of happiness, and that's what decides me.

Carefully I choose foundation, blusher, mascara, eyebrow pencil, and eye shadow. Then I pick up some herbal shampoo and conditioner. I pay with debit. I'm going through money like there's no tomorrow but I'm beyond caring.

A price list is posted on the door of Darlene's Beauty Salon in the mall. Darlene is happy to sell me a gift certificate.

Last stop is the grocery store. The makings for meat loaf join the make-up in my pack. The rain's holding off, and despite my headache, I'll make the best meat loaf ever.

Two hours later, Lorne and Seal pull into our driveway, one right after the other, and don't tell me that's coincidence. I mash the potatoes with lots of milk and butter until they're creamy. Shoes and boots hit the front mat and five minutes later they're both sitting at the table. We eat, my brother shoveling in his food like he's Abe's pig, Seal telling stories about some of his customers; you see all kinds in the liquor store.

When Lorne pushes back his chair, I say, "Hold on a minute."

He flashes his white-toothed grin. "I'm in a hurry, sis."

"Mondays and Wednesdays you'll come home for supper, which I'll cook. Six p.m. sharp. The rest of the week you can do what you like."

From sheer surprise, he drops back into his chair. "You telling me what to do?"

"Yes."

"What's going on?"

"I'm tired of you promising to come home then you end up at Sally's without even bothering to let me know." To my dismay, my voice goes raggedy. "I've got feelings, Lorne."

"Jeez, Sigrid, it's just that—"

"I don't want your excuses! I want you home twice a week. Is that too much to ask?"

I've gone from raggedy to choked-up, hurt and fury duking it out in my throat. He looks seriously alarmed. "I guess not."

"Good. Same goes for you, Seal, except when you're on late shift."

"Okay," Seal says.

Lorne's brown eyes are leveled on me now, like he's thinking hard. Underneath that, they're kind. I bet Sally goes for the kindness big time. More than for the muscles he works on at Mr. Murphy's gym?

He says, "Mom's hardly ever home, no use waiting for her to cook. Seal's got his shift work. Guess I've gotten out of the habit of coming home. Mondays and Wednesdays work for me. And how about every second Sunday I bring Sally here for supper and we'll order Chinese?"

"That'd be nice," I quaver.

"Starting this Sunday. Sorry, sis, I should've let you know the last couple days."

He pushes back his chair and this time I let him go.

Seal smooths his hair over his bald spot. He picks up his fork, looking at it like he's never seen a fork before, then starts digging it into the padded plastic place mat so it leaves rows of little dents. "Me and Davina Murphy," he says, "she lives in Ratchet and I've been seeing her."

My fingers are clenched in my lap. "I know."

"You *do?*"

"Tate told me. A while ago."

He sighs, shifts the fork to a new patch of place mat, and digs some more. "Should've known you can't spit in the ditch around here without it spreads ripples. They got us married yet?"

"Is that what you want?"

I wait for him to deny it, the blood pounding in my ears. He jabs the mat harder.

"Your mother never wanted more kids. Made that clear to me from the start. Disappointing, me never having had any of my own, but I loved her, and you and Lorne were part of the package." He looks right at me. "A good part, Sigrid. Then there was all the paperwork and phone calls from lawyers when your father asked for a divorce—she got her dander up and decided she didn't want to marry me. Common-law, that's what we settled on. I'm ruining this place mat."

He runs his thumb over the tines. "Davina and me have been chatting at Tim Hortons for a while now. Then we switched to lunches, then dinners. I want to marry her. Up front. Maybe have a kid or two."

You'll be their real dad...

"Oh," I say.

"She's a real nice woman. I'd like you to meet her."

I'm starting to hate that word *nice*. "Does my mother know?"

Another sigh, all the way from his socked feet. "Not yet." He looks up, his eyes as baffled as Mel's. "I tried to make it work with your mother—I really did. Some days, I reckon I'd have felt better if she'd had another man. But eBay and the Shopping Channel? How can you fight a frigging TV?"

The last thing I want is to feel sorry for him. I try to breathe slow. "When are you planning on telling her?"

"When I can catch her with five minutes to spare!"

"It'd better be soon. Or she'll hear it from someone else."

He picks up the fork again, stabbing it right through the plastic. "And then there's you—you've been on my mind day and night. Lorne's okay, he's a man now. But how can I move to Ratchet and leave you here alone most of the time? Last night—it scared me to realize no one was home with you all night. That's not right."

So now it's my fault he can't move in with Davina. "My mother will have to stay home more. Or Sally can come and live with Lorne. It's not your worry!"

He flinches. "Your mother and Sally might have something to say about that. Even though I'd miss you something fierce, I've wondered if you'd like to move out west, with your real father?"

The headache tightens its grip. "I'll ask him," I say coldly.

"He's been good to keep in touch and he never misses a month of his payments to Lissie."

"I'll ask him," I repeat, and push away from the table.

"I'll do the dishes. Likely you're in a hurry to go to Ratchet."

"Sigrid, I'm doing the best I can."

All the mad goes out of me, leaving me feeling sad and tired. "You gotta tell my mother, Seal. Not proper she should hear it from one of the neighbors."

"I've been putting it off. She texted me an hour ago that she's back in town...I'll head over to Ady's now." He stands up, rubbing the back of his neck, and says, real bitter, "I doubt she'll even care."

I want a hug in the worst way. Too stiff-necked to ask for one.

He says, avoiding my eyes, "After I talk to your mother, I'll tell Davina what's happening. Then I'll come straight home."

He walks out of the kitchen, and a few moments later his truck pulls out of the driveway. Once he's told my mother, everything will change.

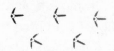

I guessed that right. She swerves into our driveway fifty minutes later, braking so hard she burns rubber. Slam of the car door, slam of the front door. Guess Lorne comes by his door-slamming honestly.

No call to be afraid of my own mother.

Rat-tat-tat of her heels on the living-room floor. She

parks herself by the kitchen door. She's vibrating with rage. "How long have you known about all this?"

She's had her hair cut, short and sassy; her denim skirt is short, too, her top a shimmer of sequins. I say carefully, "I only just found out that Seal wants to marry Davina."

"He's ruining everything! How *dare* he date someone behind my back?"

"Your back's never home."

"And what am I going to do about you when I go on buying trips? Tell Lorne he has to babysit?"

The Tylenol I took hasn't kicked in yet; my head's throbbing like someone's playing heavy metal between my ears. "I don't need a sitter."

"It's illegal for you to be alone at night. I'll tell you, Seal's buying me a brand-new computer with a 27" screen and it'll sit right here in the living room—and he'll pay me child support."

"If he does, you can afford your own computer—after all, you can afford a flashy car."

She shoots me a venomous look and starts pacing up and down the kitchen, all her movements jerky. "Ady's husband, Roy, likes us being over there. Likes his mug of tea on time and his ashtray dumped. How can it work if Ady's over here, will you explain that to me?"

I sit down hard on the nearest chair. "Ma," I say, me who never calls her anything, "when it comes to you, I can't explain my way out of a cardboard box. If you want to spend your days listening to salespeople babble about bone china, that's your problem. But don't complain if Seal wants more out of life than a wife who's addicted to bargains."

"I'm not his wife! Not to anyone but the income tax."

"Did you *ever* want to live with me?"

"I'm your mother, aren't I?"

"How would I know?"

"Course I am. Gave birth to you in St. Fabien Hospital at 5:43 on a Tuesday morning, 7 lbs. 10 oz. of squall."

"That's nearly thirteen years ago."

"So?"

Last time I cried was right here on the kitchen floor, and I won't do it again, I won't. "I'm sure you and Lorne can figure out who'll sleep home so your daughter—your daughter, Ma—isn't left alone at night. You can draw up a schedule. Post it on the refrigerator. Here and at Sally's and at Ady's."

"If your father wasn't such a deadbeat, you could live with him."

"He's good enough that you take his money!"

For a minute I think she's going to slap me, she looks so furious. "I'm going straight to Davina Murphy's place and tell her what I think of her. Her and her new boyfriend."

"Don't, Ma! Please don't do that."

But she's already halfway across the living room. I

pick up the phone, my fingers shaking, and punch in the numbers for Seal's cell. He picks up, his voice so familiar, so safe, that the rest of me starts to shake. "Hello?" he says. "Is that you, Sigrid?"

"My mother's on her way to Davina's," I say, and drop the phone back in its cradle.

Rubbing my eyes, I sit at the table until I'm sure my knees will hold me. Then I push myself upright and waver across the living room to my bedroom. The girl with the sword—what does she know about real life?

Diving under the bedspread, I pull it over my head.

TWENTY

to give

Seal taps gently on my door when he comes home. I lie still, pretending to be asleep. He opens the door, stands there a minute, then closes it. I could be a couple pillows under the bedspread for all he knows.

I stay in bed the next morning until him and Lorne have left for work. I don't have a clue where my mother spent the night. At least my headache's gone, which is a big relief.

It's time to put my second brilliant idea into action. I put the make-up I bought into a box, wrapping it in green tissue paper with a purple bow. I skip breakfast.

There's a headwind all the way to Long Bight and it's another gray day. But I have this pretty picture in my head of Mel tearing off the tissue paper, seeing all the stuff in the box, and smiling at me, an astonished smile because I cared, a sunny smile because she can make herself look more like Carly Rae Jepsen and less like Mel Corkum.

A smile that means she'll never act spitey to me again.

No truck beside Mel's place. I bang on the door.

"Comin'!" she hollers.

When she sees it's me, her mouth drops open. She should throw her t-shirt in the washer. Or the garbage.

I take the box out of its plastic bag. "This is for you."

She looks at it as if it's a live snake. "You makin' fun of me?"

I suppose it's only natural she'd act suspicious; the Shrikes were never in the habit of exchanging Christmas or birthday gifts. "It's a present, that's all."

"You got no call to be givin' me presents."

"It's nice, Mel. You'll like it."

I'm starting to feel antsy. Don't tell me I've blown it again.

She says, "You put a dead animal inside, that's what you did. Road-kill."

"I didn't!"

I thrust the box at her. She hefts it in her hand, shaking it to see if it sounds like squashed squirrel. The contents rattle. She sniffs at the tissue paper.

"See you," I say and hurry up the slope.

I can feel her eyes on my back. I'd guess it's been a very long time since anyone gave Mel Corkum a present.

After breakfast, I ride my bike to Abe's barn. He's hilling

his potatoes, and he leans on his hoe as I approach him on the path.

"Had to shovel the manure meself yesterday," he says. I blush. "Sorry."

"Hmph. Gonna rain tonight. I'll have me a good crop this year providin' I keep ahead of the beetles."

He shows me one of the brown-and-white striped beetles, squishing it between his fingers. I find a few and pass them to him. With a gap-toothed grin, he says, "You'd kill 'em, girl, if your life depended on the taters you'd stored up for winter."

Have I changed so much I don't even want to bully potato beetles?

In the barn, Ghost is on his usual perch in the loft. I talk to him for a while before I shovel the cow patties into the barrow and wheel them outside, dumping them on the manure pile. I spread fresh straw in the cow's stall, scratch the pig's back, *chuck* to the hens, then sit on a bale and pretend to fall asleep. A fly buzzes at the window. The pig snorts and the hens cluck. Will I ask my real father if I can live with him? What would it be like to move to Fort McMurray?

I'd be in the same province as Hanna.

There'd be no Seal. No Lorne.

No Hud.

No Tate. No Mel.

I hear a tiny rustle in the straw and open my eyes.

Ghost is pacing over to his food bowl. He sticks his nose in it and chows down. He's only ten feet away from me.

"Hi, Ghost," I whisper.

He freezes. "It's okay, I want to be your friend. Someday I'd like it if you came to live with me."

He darts a look over his shoulder, then bounds for the nearest bale and leaps for the loft. I can't picture him locked in a crate, flying all the way to Fort McMurray.

Abe's gone inside, so I bike home. It'll take time to tame Ghost. Can't expect to do it in three visits.

I hold onto that hope all the way to Fiddlers Cove.

Outside my place, Mel's bicycle is lying on the side of the road, and she's pounding on our front door. A plastic bag dangles from her other hand.

I stop at the end of the driveway, my heart hammering as hard as her fist. Keeping my bike between me and her, I call, "I'm over here."

Swinging the bag like a weapon, she marches over. Straight greasy hair, pale lashes, no lipstick. She thrusts the bag at me. "Open it."

She's torn the packaging off the make-up, broken the hinges on the eye shadow, and snapped the eyebrow pencil into pieces. Lipstick is smeared over the box of foundation. The gift certificate from Darlene's, for a cut and perm, is ripped in two. I can't think of a word to say, I feel that discouraged.

One more mistake to add to my total.

She sticks her face into mine. "You don't like the way I look?"

I struggle to find the right words. "Mel, I thought all girls liked make-up—I know I do. And I chose pretty colors...ones I thought you'd like."

"I asked you a question!"

"I was only trying to help."

"So you *don't* like the way I look."

"You've got it wrong," I say slowly. "The way I see it, *you* don't like the way you look."

She blinks. For a moment she looks like someone else altogether—someone sad and frightened. Someone who lost her mother. "I don't like you givin' me crappy presents," she says. "Makin' fun of me." She upends the bag. The tube of lipstick rolls down the slope and plops into the ditch. The tissue tumbles out, balled up so tight it looks like a grenade. "You leave me alone," she says. "Or I'll make *your* face look different—and it won't be with make-up."

"I'll leave you alone, Mel." I hesitate, then go for broke. "I'm sorry your mom died."

Her fist flashes out so fast that I don't have time to duck; it hits my shoulder, rocking me on my feet. She swivels on her heel, grabs her bike, and aims for Tate's place even though she's not supposed to go there. I bend down and shovel the make-up into the bag. Then I run indoors and snap every latch in the place.

I feel about as whiny as it's possible for one person to feel.

Lorne texts to say Sally's parents have invited him and Sally for supper. Seal comes home right after his shift. I made fish cakes from scratch.

As he sits down, he says, "Thanks for warning me yesterday about your mother coming to Davina's place."

And that's all he says. I wait for him to tell me how it went.

He passes me the salt, eats four fish cakes, says it's supposed to be sunny tomorrow, and gets up from the table. After he showers and changes his shirt, he says, "I'm going to Davina's. I'll be home by eleven."

I wash the dishes, dry them, put them away, wipe the counters, find the number written on the back cover of the phone book, and stare at the phone.

It's three and a half hours earlier in Fort McMurray.

In all the years since my dad left, I never once phoned him.

I tap the numbers, eleven of them. The phone rings three times before a woman's voice says, not overly polite, "Who's this?"

"Can I speak to Randy Sugden, please?"

"He's just getting out of the shower. Who's calling?"

"I'll wait," I say.

"Just a minute," she says and plunks the phone down. I can hear her talking to someone, but can't hear what she's saying.

A man says, cautious-like, "Is that you, Lissie?"

"It's Sigrid."

"Sigrid? Is something wrong?"

"No. Was that Barb who answered the phone?"

"Yeah...you can't have my letters yet because I only mailed them yesterday. One for you, one for Lorne, and one for your mother."

"Letters? What about?"

"Barb and me," he says. "We got married."

I grip the phone. "Oh. When?"

"Two days ago. Only reason I'm home is because we're taking off for the weekend, the two of us. Vegas." There's a pause. "Her sister from Edmonton is looking after the kids."

Do you still love me?

"Congratulations," I say, my voice flat as a pancake. "I hope you'll be happy."

"We get on good, me and Barb."

"That's nice."

"I'll keep on sending the money to you and Lorne, and to your mother until you turns eighteen."

"Seal's moving out."

He gives a bark of laughter. "Lasted longer than I

thought he would."

My mind goes blank. He doesn't ask what will happen to me without a dad or a stepdad.

"Our kids are doing good," he says. "They're both in school now."

"I'm your kid, too!"

"Don't I write you letters every month and me about as handy with a pen as a dog with a cod jig?"

"You could phone instead."

"S'pose I could."

"What did you do with the class picture I sent?"

He says, and you can hear the relief, "Barb framed it."

"You used to push me on our swing."

"I set one up here. Brandon—he's five—he likes it."

"I—I gotta go." I feel dizzy, like someone wound the chain on my swing real tight and now I'm whirling round and round.

"I likes getting your letters," he says gruffly. "Bye, Sigrid."

I put the phone back. If you paid me a million dollars, I wouldn't ask if I could go and live with him and his wife, Barb, and their two kids.

TWENTY-ONE

to pray

I wait until dusk before I leave the house. Black tights, black sweater, black socks, and I don't bother with a flashlight—nearest thing I own to a sword—because the Avenger's not going far.

The scrubby spruce trees behind Tate's place give me cover as I creep closer to her house. Mr. Cody's gray car is parked near the road. Mrs. Cody works late at the bookstore on Friday nights, so she's not been home long.

No light on the front porch. Blinds pulled down on one of the back windows. The other window is dimly lit. Slow as I can, I bring my head up to the sill, ready to duck and run in an instant.

The room is empty. I stand up so I can see all the way in. White walls, single bed, a bookshelf with a pile of scribblers on it but only one book: a Bible with gold lettering on the spine. It must be Tate's room.

The bedspread is brown. No rug on the floor. No pictures on the wall or ornaments on the bureau. I've never been inside a convent, but this is how I picture a nun living.

I wonder where Tate hides her chain earrings.

My shoes whispering in the grass, my shoulder tight to the siding, I creep along the side of the house. No lights in the window. I peer inside. Kitchen, and it's empty, too.

Biting my lip, I back up, shuffle behind the house, and edge along the other side where light angles over the grass because the drapes are open.

A truck approaches. Bent low, I keep my face, the only white part of me, hidden.

I should've worn a mask.

The truck drives by.

Scarce breathing, I raise my head until I can see through the gap in the curtains.

Living room. Three people in it. Mr. and Mrs. Cody, her in another of those shapeless dresses, her husband in a suit and tie. Tate's wearing plaid pajama pants and a loose t-shirt. No chains.

No one's looking my way.

Although I can't hear what Mr. Cody's saying, it's easy to see he's angry. A cold anger, his face rigid, only his lips moving. Every now and then, Mrs. Cody nods. Tate's standing very still.

Mr. Cody picks up a hardcover book from the coffee table. Tate's mother bows her head. He barks an order. Tate bows her head. He starts praying. It goes on a long time.

This isn't your normal dysfunctional family. It's Tate

smashing head-on into the Congregation of the Sacred Brotherhood.

Mel visited Tate this morning—likely barged right in even though Mrs. Cody hadn't left for work yet. Mrs. Cody must have told Mr. Cody.

My knees are stiff and a mosquito's whining by my ear. I crouch down, swat the mosquito, and wonder what I'm doing here. Another mosquito bites my neck. I squash that one, too. I should've put fly dope on. Not that I think they ever test it on real live mosquitoes. Newfie mosquitoes.

Easing my way up, I look through the window again. Mr. Cody has put the book down on the table; he's asking Tate a question. She shakes her head. He steps closer. She says something, talking fast. He raises his hand as if he's going to hit her. But he doesn't. Instead, he wraps his hand around Tate's shoulder, his wife plants both her hands on Tate's other shoulder, and together they push down hard.

Tate lands on her knees on the living-room floor. Even through the window, I can see how her father is digging his fingers into her t-shirt. Tate bows her head. Her mother and father bow their heads. The praying starts again.

I don't like this.

I should go home.

I lower myself onto the grass, squishing mosquitoes,

one of them leaving a smear of blood on my wrist. I wish the window was open so I could hear what they're saying.

Or maybe I don't.

When I stand up again, Tate's father is leaning over Tate, his fingers still rammed into her shoulder. He's short and he's skinny, but even I can see the threat. Tate's lips move. On and on. Her face is white. No expression on it.

It's a warm night and I'm cold through and through. I can't stand watching for one more second.

Bent over, I sneak behind the house. My toe stubs a rock. Even though it's almost dark, the chunks of granite that edge the lawn are paler than the grass. I look at them for a long minute.

When I pick one up, it scrapes against the next one, the noise making me jump.

No one leans out the window to see who's there.

I dig my fingers into the rock and crawl back along the side of the house. No cars or trucks on the move. A mosquito sings in my ear. Stepping away from the wall into the open, I check which windowpane doesn't have a screen, picture Mr. Cody's rigid face, take aim, and fire the rock at the window.

Smash and shatter of glass.

I'm behind the house and running hard, eyes straining to see the ground. Past our neighbors' place, then it's our place, my feet thudding on the grass. As I dart to the front door, there's not a scrap of cover. I wait for Mr. Cody to yell my name, too scared to look back and see if he's rushed outside.

Key in the lock, fingers trembling.

I slip indoors, locking the door behind me. Through my bedroom window, I look over at Tate's place. No sign of Mr. Cody and the light's still out on their front porch.

I haul off the black clothes, throw them in my closet, and pull on my PJs.

Once again, the Avenger's done her thing without thinking it through. But what choice did I have? There's times you gotta act regardless of what follows. Like calling Prinny's father when she was in the dory. Like taking on Mel and Tate when they were bullying Selena.

The Codys didn't see me. They can't possibly blame Tate for the broken window. Maybe they'll think it was Mel, who's a champion rock-thrower.

Unless they decide God fired the rock.

Tate's empty smile, her cold anger, her cruelty—now I know where she got them.

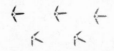

Surprise, surprise, I can't go to sleep. By now, I've convinced myself that creepy Mr. Cody will punish Tate even though she was down on her knees praying when the rock sailed through the window.

Doyle Quinn punished Hud for a flat tire.

Mel punched me for giving her a present.

Mr. Cody's anger is ice-cold, Doyle's is almost casual, while Mel's is brutal...then there's my mother, white-hot furious when all I did was fix up the kitchen, vindictive when Seal, who she doesn't want, starts dating someone else.

I wonder how she'll react when she finds out my dad has married Barb.

Rain's started pattering on the roof by the time I hear someone come in the front door. Two loud thumps. Lorne, taking off his boots. I glance at the clock, scramble out of bed, and open my door.

"Hey," he says. "How's it going?"

"You're home early."

"Sally wasn't feeling so good. Want some nachos?"

"Yeah..." I follow him into the kitchen. He takes salsa and sour cream out of the refrigerator. "I'll grate the cheese," I say.

"Want a Coke? We got any beer?"

We settle on the couch, me with pop, him with a can of Black Horse. I'm in no hurry for my first taste of beer, which in my opinion looks like pee and smells like old socks. Lorne flicks the remote to a sitcom with a lot of canned laughter.

"Lorne," I say, "do you believe in God?"

He swallows too much salsa and chokes. Wiping his eyes, he says, "I guess so...not something I think about much."

"Do you think He's mean or kind?"

Lorne lowers the volume on the TV and gives the matter some thought. That's another reason girls go for my brother—if you really want to know something, he'll do his best to come up with an answer, and not just any answer. "Not sure He's either one," he says. "If He's kind, He's not doing a great job, given the state of the world. And if He's mean...well, what's the point of having Him around?"

"D'you think we're born mean?"

"Nah. Not usually—we learn it as we go along. School's the best place."

"You're not mean."

"I can be. After we left her parents' place, Sally was right cranky. So I doled out my share of cranky until she told me it was PMS—then I rubbed her back for her and came home."

"I called Dad this afternoon. He married Barb two days ago."

"No kidding."

"They're going to Vegas for their honeymoon. Do you think he still loves us?"

"Sends us money every month."

"Guilt."

He grins. "It's still fifty bucks and they still take it at the bank."

"I never know what to say when I write to him."

"You should text, like I do. Shorter."

"Texting is for friends," I say and reach for a nacho. "Seal's dating Davina Murphy."

"Yeah, I heard. Ma's bunking at Ady and Roy's place, I heard that, too."

"Are you going to marry Sally?"

"You're some full of questions tonight. I dunno, Sigrid. I'm not ready to get hitched, I guess, and I'm none too sure Sally is. She's talking of moving to St. John's, taking French immersion, then applying for a Coast Guard course. Good money in that."

Which means you'll move to St. John's...

We watch the news. Afterward, I stack the dishes in the sink, hug my brother, and go to bed. A few minutes later, Seal comes home.

All three of us under the same roof.

TWENTY-TWO

to collide

Because Seal has an afternoon shift the next day, he wants to run a few errands in St. Fabien in the morning. He whistles softly to himself as he drives. I don't tell him my real dad married Barb, and I don't ask him how Davina's doing.

Being nice every minute of every day is too much to ask.

I take the torn gift certificate to Darlene's, where I tell the lady at the counter that the person didn't want it. I ask if I can use it for my next haircut. Although she looks like she's bursting with questions as she flattens the crinkled paper, all she says is, "Sure, dear, just make an appointment."

I pick up a couple of things at the drugstore, which makes me late for meeting Seal in Home Hardware. First person I see, staring at a row of paint cans as though they'll tell him the meaning of life, is Hud Quinn.

I don't think Flat White Latex is the answer.

I wish I knew the answer.

As I chug up and down the aisles looking for Seal, I'm

wondering why I didn't go up to Hud and say hello.

I barrel past an end display of caulking guns. Long legs in jeans, a big box with paint cans balanced on top—I see them a split second before I crash into them. The legs buckle. I try to anchor my sneaks but a boot tramps my foot, and a knee, bony as a skull, knocks me backward. The box—CERAMIC TILE 6"X 6"—tilts. The paint cans slide toward me, fast, faster. I yelp in fear, bashing into the metal shelving as I dodge.

As box and cans hit the floor with an almighty crash, an elbow spears my ribs, then my nose is buried in a plaid shirt that stinks of sweat. The guy says something short and sharp and it ain't *ouch*. He's heavy. I yelp again, a smothered yelp.

The guy pushes himself off me. The cans are rolling across the concrete floor. I gulp in air. A can of paint—Flat White Latex, I notice with a swoop of hysterical laughter—sways gently back and forth.

He says, "You little idiot—look what you did!"

Doyle Quinn. I just banged into Doyle Quinn. He's gonna belt me like he belts his son and it'll be me rolling in the aisle.

I back up fast.

It's not me I should be worried about. It's Hud. Terror rips through me. I've riled Hud's dad and guess who'll pay the price. "Sorry, sir," I mutter, bend down, and set two of the cans upright. What if the tiles are smashed?

A sales guy dashes around the corner in his red shirt with the yellow logo. "Are you all right, sir?"

"She tripped me!"

I straighten two more cans. "It was an accident. I wasn't watching where I was going...I'm real sorry."

"I'm not paying for the damage," Doyle says. "She is."

I look up at the sales guy. "I came around the corner and we collided. It all happened so fast that—"

Doyle interrupts. "You tripped me with your sneaker."

The sales guy, who's only young, says, "As long as no one's hurt, sir."

From the corner of my eye, I catch movement—Hud at the far end of the aisle. I look away because I don't want Doyle seeing him. A fair crowd's gathering. Then, to my considerable relief, I hear Seal's voice. "What's going on here? Sigrid, are you okay?"

"Stupid little—" Doyle stops dead, probably deciding that swearing at me isn't the best way to go. "She did it on purpose. Banged into me and wrecked all this stuff."

"I didn't," I wail. "It was an accident."

"Calm down, Sigrid," Seal says, and looks at the sales guy. "Will the store make good the damage?"

"Yes sir, we're insured against accidental damage of goods in-store."

"In that case, Doyle," Seal says, his voice like cracked ice, "there's no problem. You replace what's broken and head on your way. And leave my stepdaughter alone."

He puts an arm around my shoulders. There's a low murmur of approval from the crowd. Hud has disappeared.

Doyle gives me a look that would blister skin. Nothing cold about his anger. Still, give me Doyle Quinn over Mr. Cody any day of the week, which is a weird thought to have when I could have ended up *splat* on the concrete floor.

Seal leads me away. When we're out of earshot of everyone else, he says, "Okay, what was that all about?"

"It really was an accident—I was late getting here, so I was rushing along looking for you and collided with him and his stupid tiles. I never would have done it on purpose, Seal, not to Doyle Quinn. He beats on his son. For no reason. In school, you often see Hud with bruises."

Seal frowns at me. "I've lived here for years and I've never seen him hit Hud. If he did, though—"

"If? You think I'm making this up?"

"Domestic violence is a matter for the cops. And you'd need witnesses."

"You remember the morning you helped Doyle with his flat? He beat Hud up for that, and it wasn't Hud's fault."

"I'll keep my eyes open," Seal says. "And you tell me if you see Doyle do anything to Hud, okay?"

"You saw how angry Doyle was," I say in a small voice. "Likely Hud's in trouble already."

"I'll ask around, see what I can find out. But there's no point fretting about it, Sigrid." He tousles my hair. "I still have to go to the bank. What about you?"

"I might look for a pair of shorts."

"How about I meet you by the mall entrance in half an hour?"

I push through the mall doors and walk past the teachers' supply store and Darlene's. How can I concentrate on shorts when I feel sick to my stomach?

Which suddenly lurches. Hud has Travis backed into a corner beside the video store.

It'd look innocent to someone who doesn't know Hud. I pick up my pace.

Hud's got Travis in a wristlock. While Travis has grown the last couple months, he's still a lot shorter than Hud. But he's not cringing like Vi or Selena. Travis has attitude.

I say casually, "Hi, guys. Hud, you gotta minute?"

Travis kicks Hud hard on the ankle. As Hud drops Travis's wrist, Travis whips past both of us. Hud takes a step after him, stops, and glares at me. "Get lost!"

"When are you going to quit being a bully? You're worth more than that."

"You're like a reformed smoker—now that you've quit, the whole world has to quit."

"I hate seeing your mean side."

"Deal with it," he says. "It's all there is."

I put my hands on my hips. "That's such crap."

"You're living in la-la land. I *like* bullying."

The words come from deep inside. "Once you let your mean side off the leash, it runs you."

He jams his thumbs in the pockets of his jeans. His t-shirt is rumpled, like he left it in the dryer still damp. "You should know. You tripped my dad."

"It was an accident, Hud! I was in a hurry and I didn't see him until it was too late."

"Making a fool of him like that—he'll be seriously pissed."

I grab at hope like a drowning man grabbing a stick of kindling. "You didn't collide with him. Why would he take it out on *you?*"

"Were you born dumb? Or do you work at it every day?"

I'm shivering, and it's nothing to do with the air-conditioning in the mall. "The minute those paint cans started rolling across the floor, I knew you were in trouble."

"No fun leaving la-la land, is it, Sigrid?"

"I'm *sorry* I banged into him...I don't understand how he can beat you up when you haven't done one thing to provoke him."

"Me living in the same house provokes him."

"Maybe you were adopted," I say wildly. "Maybe your mother got pregnant by somebody else and that's why he hates you."

"Grow up! I got his eyes and his build and his dark hair. And you think my mother would dare step out of line?"

"I'm the one who put nails in your driveway so his tire would go flat."

I sure hadn't planned on saying that.

Hud looks blank, as though I've just confessed to first-degree murder. The silence—except for the mall's sappy music—is more than I can take. "I did it the day I saw him hit you, his fist cracking into your face and you taking it as though it wasn't anything to get excited about. I sneaked out of the house once everyone was in bed. Used some of Seal's roofing nails." I bite my lip. "I didn't understand that he'd—I'm so sorry, Hud."

I never realized what a wishy-washy word *sorry* is.

Slowly Hud's eyes re-enter real time. "He thrashed me for that," he says with as much feeling as if he was talking about the weather. "Stay outta my life, Sigrid. You do more damage than a truckload of paint cans."

"No," I say.

Doyle flashes across his face, that red-hot rage. "I'm warning you—back off."

My heart racketing away, I say, "You're my friend, and friends stick together."

Astounded, he says, "You coming onto me? You're too young."

Cheeks on fire, I cry, "You're the only person in school who'll talk to me—doesn't that make you a friend?"

"How would I know?"

"Well, I figure it does."

"You know what?" he says. "You remind me of Travis. He comes out with the weirdest stuff, too, and he never knows when to back off."

I guess this is a compliment. Should I say *thank you?* But before I can say anything, Hud's face changes.

"Dad's coming," he says, fear cracking his voice. "If he sees you and me—git!"

Praying that Doyle hasn't seen us, praying that Hud will be okay, I scurry into the video store. DVDs and war games. Guns and blood. No matter what I do, things go to the bad.

I edge past a rack of body-builder videos, then peer out the door. Hud and his dad are leaving the mall, Hud three steps behind, his skinny shoulders hunched.

Not a thing I can do.

I don't have the heart to buy shorts, so I sit on a bench by the mall entrance and wait for Seal. A few minutes later, he walks up to me, smiling, holding out a plastic bag. "Look what I found in the Dollar Store."

It's a red china soap dish, nicer than the one Tate smashed. My eyes fill with tears. "Seal, I don't want you to move out."

He sits down next to me and puts an arm around my shoulders. "C'mon, Sigrid—I won't just walk out the door and abandon you."

"I phoned my real dad...he got married this week. Didn't bother to invite me or Lorne." I stare at a dried-up wad of bubblegum stuck to the floor. "His new wife wasn't real friendly to me on the phone."

"Oh...guess you won't want to be moving out there, then." Lines crease Seal's forehead, deep lines. "Don't worry, we'll figure something."

"I love the dish," I quaver. "Thank you."

"Let's eat at Subway," he says.

"Okay." I get up and give him a quick hug, knowing how lucky I am.

I can't bear to think what's happening to Hud right now.

TWENTY-THREE

to weep

Seal drives to work after he drops me off at home. Lorne's at the garage all day. After I clean the bathroom, I carefully put a new bar of soap in the soap dish. Then I stare at my face, my ordinary face, in the mirror.

How will I find out what's happened to Hud?

I prop myself on the couch for a while and try to read; I wash the kitchen floor; I make a broccoli-and-cheese casserole that I can reheat with leftover fish cakes when Seal comes home for supper. Finally, I can't stand it any longer. I wheel my bike out of the garage and pedal down the road. I don't even bother to watch for Tate.

Doyle's truck isn't outside Hud's place. I knock on their screen door. Footsteps shuffle down the hall. Through the wire mesh, Hud's mother says, "Yes?"

She's wearing a pale blue blouse and navy slacks, both newly ironed. Her hair is clean. But her face—whoever lives behind it went away a long time ago, with no plans to return.

"Hi, Mrs. Quinn," I say, "is Hud home?"

"He's gone on his bike."

"Which way?"

She points in the general direction of Ratchet.

I smile at her. "Thank you," I say, and take off in the same direction.

In Ratchet, I slow down, my knuckles white on the handlebars as I search for Hud.

The third mailbox past Prinny's place jumps out at me. Decorated with birds and yellow daisies, it has DAVINA MURPHY printed on the flap. A small blue car is parked by the porch of her bungalow, which is painted green with white trim. The garden is full of flowers in drifts of pink, white, and purple. Lilac plumes scent the air.

Like I'm in a dream, I walk up the driveway. The door is purple, too, with a wooden sign fixed to it, morning glories curling around letters that spell WELCOME.

I raise my knuckles to knock. Then I lower them.

What if she doesn't want me here?

I'm the reason her and Seal can't move in together.

I turn on my heel, run back to my bike, and take off down the road.

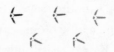

When I reach Abe's barn, I lean my bicycle against the fence and walk up the path. He's not around, and neither are Prinny or Travis. With a sigh of relief, I sit on my bale of hay and lean back. I need some down-time before

I find Hud. I've just seen a house that's a home, a real home, a home that'll never be mine.

Ghost is perched on the crossbeam. We pretend we're ignoring each other.

For a while, my thoughts chase each other in circles. But as the pig grunts, the hens cluck, and little specks of dust wander through the air, I start to feel better.

Ghost jumps down the hay bales, keeping as far from me as he can, and shoves his nose in his dish. "Hi there," I say softly. His tail jerks. "You gonna be my friend? There's not exactly a line-up for the job."

He stops eating and looks over his shoulder at me, big yellow eyes with dark centers. "We've got all summer," I say. "No rush."

He chows down again. Then, like it's becoming part of our routine, he walks outside through the gap in the wall.

A few minutes later, I follow him outside. I can't put off finding Hud any longer.

I head further east, toward Gulley Cove, and there he is on his rock, staring out to sea.

He knows that I know it's his favorite place. So is he waiting for me? Or is he here because where else can he go to lean into the horizon?

I've been barging into people's lives right and left and where's it got me? I'm going to leave him alone for once. I needed alone-time in the barn. Why wouldn't he need the same?

Or am I being a coward?

So fast it startles me, three ravens swoop from below the cliffs and fly right at me. My bike scrapes the dirt. The ravens veer over my head.

Hud looks over his shoulder.

Stupid to leave now. *Dumb,* to use his word. Gripping the handlebars, I walk closer.

He stands up. There's a nasty bruise on his cheekbone that wasn't there at the mall. It's purple, like Davina's door.

Without any warning, tears start pouring down my cheeks. An ugly, snorting sob bursts out of me. I'm so horrified, so mortified, I try to turn my bike around. But I stumble over a rut because I can't see where I'm going, cliffs, road, and Hud all blurred together.

He says, "What are *you* crying for?"

My bike clanks to the ground. I sit down hard in the dirt, head on my knees, rocking back and forth as sobs clog my throat, sore and raspy. Behind my eyes, everything's blacker than black.

An arm lands on my shoulder. Rough, like he's gonna push me into the dirt. I flinch. But then his other arm goes around me. Edgy, as if I might break. He says, sounding desperate, "Don't cry—I'm not worth crying for."

I burrow into him, my forehead bumping his collarbone, and the sobs keep coming. "All I d-do...is m-make everything...worse. I'm *s-sorry.*"

"It's okay. If it hadn't been you, he'd have found another reason to hit me."

"But that's t-terrible."

I'm sniffing and snuffling by now, in desperate need of a Kleenex. Hud doesn't strike me as the type to carry Kleenex.

I don't want him to let go.

Loud and sharp, a girl's voice says, "What's going on? Hud, what are you doing to her?"

Hud jerks. I look up. Prinny's standing there, outlined by the sun like an avenging angel. Laice is behind her. They're both straddling their bikes.

"Nothing!" Hud says.

"Why's she crying?"

"Dunno," he says.

"Because," I say.

He gets to his feet and holds out his hand. I take it and pull myself up, and because I like the feel of his hand, I hold on. Prinny's looking from him to me and back again.

She came to my defense. It wasn't needed, but it's gotta count.

Laice is looking at me as though I've got snot on my face. Which I have. I snuffle some more. Prinny digs in her pocket and passes me a small wad of tissues.

"Thanks," I say, letting go of Hud's hand and blowing my nose.

Then I say, my eyes on Prinny, my voice still hitching,

"Hud's my buddy. I was crying because I keep screwing up other people's lives—his in particular. As if I'm still a Shrike, still part of Tate and Mel. I *can't* quit! No matter how hard I try."

Once you let your mean side off the leash, it runs you.

Prinny says, "You stopped Tate and Mel from stealing Selena's money outside the cafeteria."

She says it like she's reciting the words off a piece of paper the teacher handed her in class.

Just as stiff, I say, "Thank you for speaking up just now, when you thought Hud was bullying me. That was nice of you."

She nods. Then she and Laice climb on their bikes and take off to Gulley Cove.

I say, scuffing my toe in the dirt, "Well, she's sure sitting on the fence. Hud, I swear I'll never go within five miles of your dad again and you *are* worth crying for."

He starts scuffing with his toe, too. The pair of us, digging holes in the road. "It's only a bruise," he says.

"When it comes to bruises, there isn't any *only.*"

"You arguing again?" But he says it with the beginnings of a smile.

How can he smile? I blink back another rush of tears. "What your dad does, it's awful and it's wrong—"

And then I'm stumbling through all the other reasons I couldn't stop crying—my dad who left home and never came back, my stepdad who wants to live with Davina Murphy, Mel whose dad misses his dead wife, Tate whose dad prays over her like he wants God to send her straight to Hell...

My breath is still catching in my throat. "Is this rock the place you come when it's all too much and you don't know what to do?"

"Yeah," Hud says, scuffing away.

"I go to Abe's barn. I'm trying to tame the white cat that lives there. His name is Ghost."

Hud's body jolts, like I just ploughed him with my fist. The bruise stands out livid on his cheek. "What white cat?"

"It used to live in Gulley Cove."

"Why are you shoving that cat in my face?"

"Huh? What are you talking about?"

"Last fall—it was in a cage and I was gonna drown it, cage and all."

My turn to go pale. "I didn't know that."

He gives me his blank stare. In a horrible way it reminds me of Tate's empty smile. He snarls, "You sure get under my skin."

Ticks get under people's skin. And leeches.

"I dunno anything about you and the white cat," I say, "although if you were trying to drown him, no wonder he's a mess of nerves."

"So no one ever said?"

I frown at him. "Tate collects dirt the length of the shore and she's never mentioned it."

"How weird is that," Hud says slowly, staring over my shoulder at the sea.

I don't have a clue what he means and there's no point asking. "You know what? You gotta stop all this bullying. Picking on helpless cats, punching guys like Travis."

"The perfect Travis Keating."

"Travis isn't perfect, he's just decent!"

Hud takes two steps back, as if breathing the same air as me will contaminate him. Then he strides over to his rock, yanks his bike out of the grass, and pedals down the road to Ratchet as though every guy he's ever bullied is on his tail.

I sit down in the middle of the road again. Another raven swoops into the air, like it's playing, like it's having fun.

A bucket-load of tears and I feel worse, not better.

TWENTY-FOUR

to question

At home, I fall into bed and sleep until suppertime. Seal and me eat fish cakes and broccoli casserole, then he leaves right after we do the dishes. "I won't be late," he says, like him being home early will fix all our problems. He still hasn't told me how the threesome went—him, Davina, and my mother.

I can't settle to anything. It's one of those evenings when I wish Hanna was here, the music blaring and us dancing until we drop.

The barn. Makes sense that the more I go, the quicker Ghost will get used to me.

Ghost, the cat Hud tried to drown...

There's a bicycle propped against Abe's fence. A boy's bicycle. Abe's hoeing the garden. He leans on the handle. "Hard for Travis to get a minute to hisself, what with Prinny, Laice, and now you."

"I want to ask him a question."

"You go right ahead." He spits into the little ditch between the rows. "You're better off chasin' Travis than the likes of your buddy Hud Quinn."

So is that what Hud is? My buddy?

I stick my nose in the air and march to the barn. When the door creaks open, Ghost leaps for the loft. Travis looks around. "Hey, Sigrid."

"Sorry I scared the cat. Are you gonna adopt him?"

"Nah. Just trying to tame him."

He's sitting on my bale of straw. I sit on the next one over. "Did you know that Hud tried to drown Ghost in a cage?"

"Where did you hear that?"

"He told me."

"He did?" Travis tugs his ear. "Yeah, I knew. I was there. It was a while ago—one day last winter when I was at Gulley Cove. He was kicking the cage with the cat inside. Told me he was going to drown Ghost."

"And you *stopped* him?"

"Tripped him so he fell into the sea."

"No wonder he hates you." I shred an end of straw. "He figures you told everyone."

Travis shrugs. "He hated me way before that and what's the good of tattling?"

"I tripped Hud's dad at Home Hardware. By accident. He took it out on Hud even though Hud had nothing to do with it. Have you ever seen Doyle hit Hud?"

"Twice."

"You *have?* Has Prinny? Or Laice?"

"Dunno. You'd have to ask them."

I wonder if the Herbey girls ever have, or Buck and Cole. Or Tate. "I saw him, too...a few days ago. Do cops listen to kids?"

Travis's eyes narrow. "What's up?"

If you want someone to be your friend, you tell them stuff, right? You trust them. I remember the girl in the poster, holding her sword high.

I say slowly, "If I could find other people who saw Doyle hit Hud...if we went to the cops with the names... would that help Hud or would it make it worse? I have to tell you, my record for making things worse stands at 110%."

"Hard to know with someone like Doyle. I never told anyone I saw him hit Hud."

"If I ask around, can I talk to you again in a few days?"

"Sure," he says.

I smile at him, a big smile because it's good to have an ally. "Thanks, Travis...I've been trying to tame Ghost, too."

"Good luck," he says, and smiles right back.

I wish Prinny would smile at me like that.

Outside, Abe's hoeing away. I might as well make a start. "Abe, did you ever see Doyle Quinn hit Hud?"

"Nope. Can't say I'd get too flustered if I did."

"Doyle's real mean and Hud's not as bad as you think!"

"*Hmph*," says Abe.

Discouraged, I trudge down the path. But I stop off at Prinny's place on the way through Ratchet; she's Hud's first cousin. She and Laice are sitting on a new wooden swing beside the house, the two of them chatting away, and I feel a stab of such envy that my steps falter. When they see me, they go quiet.

I say, "Did either of you ever see Doyle Quinn hit Hud?"

Prinny says slowly, "My Uncle Doyle is one mean cuss, and I've seen bruises on Hud. But I never actually saw my uncle hitting him. What about you, Laice?"

"No," Laice says.

"Will you keep your eyes open? And let me know?"

Prinny gives me the same narrow-eyed look as Travis. "Okay," she says.

I leave them to it. Today seems to have gone on for a very long time, and I want to be home in my own place, with my new bedspread and my two posters on the wall. I bike along the road, sea on one side, barrens on the other, wondering if right now one of those birds called shrikes is jabbing its prey onto a thorn.

Back in Fiddlers Cove, the first person I see is Tate sitting on her front steps, her arms looped around her knees, her gaze fastened on the clipped grass of the lawn. She looks...lonesome.

Am I out of my mind?

Her father reading from his prayer book when he looked as if he'd rather drop it on her head...him and his wife forcing Tate to her knees... I'd like to paint *God Isn't Mean* in big red letters on their gray car. But I won't. Because guess who'd be blamed and it wouldn't be me.

As I turn into her driveway and drop my bike on the grass, she looks up and springs to her feet. "Tate," I say, "have you ever seen Doyle Quinn hit Hud?"

Chopping off her words, she says, "Someone fired a rock through our window last night. It was you, wasn't it? Paying me back for tripping you on the school steps."

I look puzzled. "Rock? What rock?"

"Ten o'clock last night, you broke our living-room window. With a rock."

"Any rock-throwing done around here, it's Mel."

"It wasn't Mel!"

"It sure wasn't me," I say with just the right touch of impatience. "So tell me—have you ever seen Doyle Quinn hit Hud?"

"Maybe," she says.

"Yes or no?"

"You got a thing going for Hud?"

"I saw Doyle hit him one day last week. I want to know who else has seen him."

"Twenty bucks and I might tell you," she says. "Thirty ups your chances."

I take a deep breath. "I told Hud he should quit bullying because he's worth more than that. So are you."

"Proper little do-gooder, aren't you?"

"You and me...we could be friends."

"Don't make me laugh."

My tongue spouts four small words. "I threw that rock."

There's a moment of dead silence. "What did you do that for?"

"I was watching through the window and saw how your parents treat you. Praying that looked like cursing."

"You *spied* on me?"

Because she's standing on the bottom step, she's taller than me. My sword feels like a big weight but I lift it anyway. "It's not right, what they were doing. There's all kinds of *mean,* and that was the worst I ever saw."

"I'm gonna make you real sorry you looked through that window."

"I was trying to help!"

"I don't need your help! When I'm done with you, you're the one who'll need help."

"You could do with a friend," I say. Leaning down, I grab my bike and ride home.

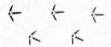

The next day's Sunday, all day. I lie in, gazing at the white cat on my poster, wondering how Hud could kick a cage with a cat inside. *Would* he have drowned the cat? Could he have been that mean?

I shoved two cats into a nor'easter. Me, Sigrid Sugden, who never had a dad who beat me.

I look at the girl, her silver sword. Maybe a sword's a bad idea. It's a weapon, after all. Something you scare people with, like we used to scare kids in school—Mel with her big fists, Tate with her scary voice, me with my smartphone.

My phone stays in my pocket these days; but the rest of me is a disaster waiting to happen.

In the afternoon, I shovel manure at Abe's and talk to Ghost. Then I make myself visit the Herbeys, as well as Buck, Cole, and Stevie. None of them ever saw Doyle hit Hud. All of them look at me like I've turned into an alien.

If it's only Travis and me as witnesses, I doubt the cops'll pay much attention.

I go home and lay the table, using a tablecloth from the linen cupboard, and folding cloth napkins so they stand up in triangles. Lorne phones in our order for Chinese food and goes to pick it up, bringing Sally back with him. She's real nice, pleased to be with Lorne and pleased to meet us. Seal holds up his end. But he'd be happier if Davina was here, I know he would be.

He can't ask Davina to supper in a house that belongs to my mother.

At least my mother didn't sniff out the Chinese food and turn up on the doorstep.

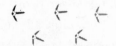

I walk up the road to check the mailbox early Monday morning. Mel's bike is thrown on the lawn at Tate's.

How can Tate risk a repeat of that awful praying?

Two bills are in the box along with a letter from my dad, his scrawly handwriting on the envelope. I open it in my room with the door shut even though no one's home but me. A photo of him in a suit and tie with a tall, dark-haired woman in a flowered dress. Barb. She's laughing, her hand tucked into his elbow, him smiling down at her. In the second photo, my dad's holding two tow-headed little boys, one on each arm. All three of them laughing.

I read the letter, once, twice, although it doesn't tell me much I didn't already know. In the envelope, there's a fifty-dollar bill.

One of the new ones, with a Coast Guard boat chugging through chunks of ice.

TWENTY-FIVE

to trample

Mel's bike is still outside Tate's when I leave for Ratchet, where I plan to ask Hector Baldwin if he's ever seen Doyle in action. Doing something—anything—is better than sitting around feeling sorry for myself. I'll check Danny Grimsby later on. Not that he'd be much use when it comes to cops, him being plastered most of the time.

I should be asking Mel. She used to come to Fiddlers Cove a fair bit when the three of us were a team.

Thinking about the Shrikes, the team of three, makes me shrivel with shame.

Hector's mom answers the door, nattering on like she hasn't spoken to another living soul in weeks. Hector comes out on their front step and shuts her off by closing the door. I ask my usual question.

"Yeah," he says.

"Yeah? You mean you saw Doyle hit Hud?"

"Mom was driving me to the dentist." He frowns in thought. "September. Before Travis arrived."

"Did she see?"

He shakes his head.

I tell him my plan about the cops, and he says he'd go if we did. "Thanks, Hector, that's great," I say, smile at him, and get a grunt in return.

I'm back on the road, wondering what to do next, when Davina's car passes me and turns up her driveway. My heart starts thumping away.

She carries three bags of groceries into the house. Car door still open. I push my bike up her driveway. Early roses in the garden. Bees circling some spiky pink flowers. Pretty lace curtains in the windows.

She comes out of the house again. She's wearing a flowered skirt with a pink top, not a rhinestone or sequin in sight. She's not pretty until she smiles, then it's like the sun came out. "Hello," she says. "You're Sigrid, aren't you?"

"How'd you know?"

"Seal showed me pictures. Want to give me a hand with the groceries?"

Her kitchen is sparkling clean, needlepoint pictures on the walls, herbs growing in pots on the windowsill. She says, "I'll pour some iced tea once I've put the groceries away."

"Was my mother really awful the day she came here?" I blurt.

"She wasn't very pleasant. But, you know, it's obvious she stopped loving Seal a long time ago."

There's something about her face, it makes you trust

her right away. "Seal's a great stepdad. He told me he wants to marry you. But my mother is scarcely ever home and he can't leave me alone in the house at night."

She stops on her way to the pantry, a package of Tostitos—Seal's favorite—in her hand. "Don't worry about it, Sigrid. We'll work something out."

"But—"

"Seal loves you. Seal and me love each other. I don't know about love moving mountains, but it can move you, me, and Seal, sure."

The thing is, I believe her.

She finds out I haven't had lunch yet. We have ham sandwiches, iced tea, sliced apple, and sugar cookies, and we talk like we've known each other a long time. She tells me about Barley, her first husband—*I missed him sore when he died*—and I tell her how I'm trying to change my ways and how difficult it is. She listens, taking it all in, and I wish with all my heart she could be my stepmother even though I know my own mother would throw a hissy fit at the thought.

She hugs me when I leave, and I hug her back. I'm near to crying, I feel so happy, so hopeful. My feet dance themselves down her driveway.

It's time to do my barn chores. Seal won't be back for a couple of hours, and there's leftover Chinese for supper.

Maybe my happiness will rub off on Ghost, and he'll

sit in my lap and purr because he's happy, too. Dream big. Why not?

Abe's truck is gone. I leave my bike by the fence. In the barn, Ghost is sitting near the pen where the hens come in and out. He tenses when he sees me, his haunches bunched to make a leap for the loft. I stop by the door, speaking to him real soft, not moving a muscle. He sticks out one back leg and lashes it with his tongue, like being clean is all that's on his mind. Then he goes back to watching the hens.

"You better not try catching one of them," I say, stepping slow and careful toward my bale of straw. "Abe won't give you any more cow milk if you do, and are you ever going to let me pick you up?"

Ghost washes his other back foot. I scratch the pig between the ears, then I sit down, leaning my head back. Davina's kitchen settles into my mind, her so friendly and nice, how easy she was to talk to....

The barn door creaks open. Hoping it's Travis, I open my eyes.

"Hello, Sigrid," Tate says.

Mel fires a stone at Ghost, hitting him on the shoulder. He screeches, short and sharp. As she runs at him, shouting and waving her arms, he streaks out his little door. I'm on my feet. I dart past Tate. Mel seizes me by the arm and swings me around. I kick her shin, all the fury from that screech behind my muscles.

"Hold onto her, Mel!" Tate cries.

Mel hauls my arm up my back. I struggle anyway, drowning pain in rage. "How'd you know where to find me?"

"We been following you on Mel's bike. Took your time at Davina's, didn't you?"

She marches to the chickens' pen, kicks at the wooden struts, and drags on the wire. The hens flap their wings and rush outside, squawking. Holding one end of a strut, she brings her heel down on it. It breaks in two. She tramples the wire to the ground, then overturns the food and water dishes.

I croak, "Are you crazy?"

"I told you I'd make you pay for spying on me," she says, smashing another strut.

"Abe will be home any minute."

"No, he won't. He's at Danny Grimsby's. They'll crack open the rum and that's them done."

With a sweep of her hand, she knocks the plastic bottle of treats off the shelf. *The pantry, bottles of ketchup and mustard crashing to the floor...*

She opens the barn door wide. She opens the pig's wooden gate. Then she climbs his fence and kicks him once, twice. He oinks, turning his head, and if a pig can show disbelief, this pig does. I go limp in Mel's grip, like I've given up, like it's all over.

Instead of falling for it, she pulls my arm higher. Pain

screams from my shoulder. She says, "I'm here because I didn't like your present."

There's an old stick leaning against one of the beams. Tate picks it up and wallops the pig across the backside. With a sound between a snort and a bleat, he runs through the open door of his pen to the big rectangle of light that's the barn door. His hoofs scrabble across the wooden floor, and he's gone.

Tate does her best to overturn the feed barrel, gasping with effort.

As Mel's hands slacken for a moment, I elbow her in the gut and throw myself forward and I almost make it, I'm almost free. She stomps her big foot on mine, anchoring me, then locks her arms around my waist. I'm helpless as a hen and so furious I'm surprised the whole barn doesn't burst into flames.

"Outside," Tate says, abandoning the barrel.

Mel half-lifts, half-hauls me over the threshold, me fighting her every inch of the way. The pig is rooting in the garden. Tate starts stamping on the row of beans, their little green leaves so new and fresh.

"Don't, Tate!"

Mel drags me closer to the garden. No one around, no use yelling for help. When Tate starts on the potatoes, kicking at the clusters of green leaves, so carefully hilled, the pig runs for cover into the tall grass on the far side of the garden. She yanks on the wire holding the pea stems with their curls of green, rips the plants out of the ground, and flings them to one side.

Mel says, "Learning your lesson, Sigrid?"

The long row of beet greens with their dark pink stems get trampled under Tate's feet, then the feathery carrot leaves. Mud's clinging to her sneakers. Abe must have watered the garden this morning, and somehow this makes it worse.

Abe trusted me. Tate and Mel wouldn't be here if I hadn't interfered in their lives.

The garden's a wreck, crushed leaves, stems broken and already wilting. Then Tate runs to the gate that opens onto the road and shoves it wide open. Back up the hill, she unties the cow from the post and leads her down the slope. The cow plods after her, her udder swaying, her long tail switching the flies.

I twist and squirm. "Stop it, Tate! You can't do that, you *mustn't*—it's dangerous."

On the other side of the road, sharp-edged rocks, then a steep drop to the sea.

Tate leads the cow to the middle of the road, unhitches the rope, and loops it around her arm. Then she runs for my bike, hollering, "Let Sigrid go, Mel! We've done all we can here—time to leave."

Mel drops me and lumbers down the slope. I race past her. I have to reach the cow before Mel takes it in her head to throw stones at her and send her over the cliff.

The cow sees me coming, gives a low moo, and trundles closer to the edge of the road. I stop dead. Can't risk driving her on to the rocks. Over my shoulder, as if it's happening to someone else, I see Tate drive away on my bike and Mel on hers. They disappear around the corner.

I'm alone in the middle of the road with a cow. I've never been this close to a cow before. I hadn't realized how big they are.

The pig could get out, too. But if I shut the gate, I can't drive the cow through it.

In a shaky voice, I say, "Nice cow, good cow," and reach for the rope halter. She tosses her head. Pink lips with pale whiskers. Dark, curvy eyelashes in a wide brown face.

Okay, Sigrid. You don't need a sword here. You need brains.

If I go around her back end, I'll be between her and the rocks. Cautiously, I step past her hip, her bones big as whalebones. Her tail swishes, its white tuft walloping me on the thigh. I yelp. She takes a startled step forward. We both stand there, frozen.

"I gotta get you in the field," I whisper. "Please, help me out."

Am I praying to a cow now?

Making as wide a circle as I can, I walk around her tail. Then I try twice more to catch hold of her halter, taking my time, talking to her soft like I talk to Ghost, wishing I could close my mind to Ghost. One stone undoing all of Travis's taming and mine.

The third time, my fingers brush the halter, but the cow jerks her head so sharp I can't get a grip.

I step back, breathe deep, and talk to her some more.

Then, from behind me, I hear sounds. Bike tires in the dirt, someone panting. It can't be Tate, it's the wrong way, the way from Gulley Cove.

Hud crests the hill, knees and elbows sticking out.

When he sees me and the cow, he brakes so sudden that the bike slews in the dirt.

The cow skitters sideways, almost on top of me and the rocks. Heart thudding, I back up as far as I can go. The whites of her eyes catching the light, she makes an ungainly hop away from me, then stands still, her sides heaving. She lifts her tail. Wet and stinky, a cow pattie plops to the road.

Hud puts his bike down. He walks alongside the cow, keeping his distance, ending up several feet from her pink nose, and all the while he's checking out the open gate, the pig rooting happily in the ruined garden, the wide-open barn door.

'What happened?" he says, and he sounds almost awestruck.

"What d'you think happened? Tate and Mel." I wipe my hands down my jeans. "Unless you think *I* did it?"

"Hey, take it easy."

"'Cause if you think *that*, there's no use pretending we're friends."

"Chill out, Sigrid! I know you didn't do it. You're too much of a softie."

A *softie?* "Chill out? Take it easy? When a cow's on the loose?"

"The pig, too," he says.

My voice as jagged as the rocks, I say, "We have to lead the cow into Abe's field before someone comes along and she ends up breaking a leg. Or falling down the cliff."

We...like I'm counting on Hud to help.

When he steps nearer, the cow backs up, her big hooves scraping the dirt, slobber dangling in long strands from her lips.

I take a couple of deep breaths. Maybe *chill out* wasn't such bad advice. "You stay here, Hud. I'll get some grass. Likely we can lead her through the gate that way."

I dash across the road, tear big handfuls of grass mixed with clover and daisies out of the ditch, and hurry back.

"Do cows eat daisies?" Hud says dubiously.

"Sure they do," I say, as if I know all about the eating habits of cows.

Standing close to him, I pass him the ragged green bundle. He pulls out a couple of daisies and drops them on the ground, and that's when we both hear the same sound—a vehicle coming from the direction of Ratchet.

Surely whoever it is will help us.

Abe's rattletrap old truck comes around the bend. Its brakes squeal. Louder than Ghost, I think, ice congealing in my belly.

The cow throws her head back and moos.

Twenty-Six

to snare

Abe climbs out of his truck. to the ground. Taking his time, he looks from us and the cow to the pig happily tromping what's left of the garden. Then he fastens his faded blue eyes on me. "I warned you against keepin' company with Hud."

"Huh?" I say stupidly.

"I put my trust in you. And now look what your buddy's done."

Hud takes a step forward. "I didn't do it!"

Abe ignores him. "And where was you, Sigrid, while all this was goin' on? Did you stand and watch? Or did you arrive after he was done, so you decided to have a nice chat, the two o' you, and me cow standin' this close to the rocks?"

"Did I stand and watch?" I say in a thin voice. "Is *that* what you think of me?"

"I tol' you the day we had our talk about you visitin' the barn that I don't much hold with change."

I can't come up with one flicker of anger. Not one. Not even when I need it so bad. I force my brain in gear. "It

214

wasn't Hud...it was two other girls."

"Two other girls," Abe says. "I don't see no other girls."

"They left. On bikes."

"No cause to lie, just to defend the likes of Hud Quinn."

"I'm telling you the truth!"

Abe turns to Hud. "I seen you in action before, and none of it good. But me cow? The pig? The garden?"

"It was Tate and Mel," Hud says, real fierce, "and I'd bet you six cows Sigrid did her best to stop them."

"Ain't you a fine pair," Abe says.

He turns away, walks up to the cow, and strokes her long nose, his movements calm and gentle. "Okay, Rosie, settle down now. Proper thing Danny was dead-drunk, seeing as how it made me come home early."

As he takes her by the halter, she stands there, placid as can be. Abe says, "Where's the rope?"

"One of the girls took it," I say.

He sighs. "I s'pose this young feller tossed it over the cliff."

"I never saw the rope!"

"Hud came along after," I cry, "he was only trying to help. Truly, Abe, I *did* try to stop them—I love your barn, I wouldn't touch anything in it."

"You won't get the chance again because neither one of you will be comin' anywheres near my place—not you nor him," Abe says. Then he leads the cow across the road and up the sloping path toward the garden.

I've never been beaten up in my life—Mel's the closest I've come to that—but I figure this is how you might feel after someone puts his fists to you.

I don't say this to Hud. He's scowling at Abe's back. "He didn't even listen to you. Tate and Mel—I'm gonna clean their clock."

"Bit late for that."

He shifts the scowl to my face. "You going home now?"

"No," I say, my shoulders sagging. "Mel threw a rock at the white cat, scared it silly so it high-tailed out of the barn—I'm worried it might be lost, or too frightened to come back for food. So I guess I'll go up the road a piece, then search the woods behind the barn." The words burst out of me. "Does *mean* always win?"

"Seems like it." His eyes are gray as the sea in winter. "No use me searching for the white cat."

"Thanks for sticking up for me."

"You stuck up for me, too. For all the good it did."

"I'm no softie. Whatever that is."

"It was a compliment!"

My first compliment from a guy and it sounds like an insult? I say, thinking my way, "Maybe, underneath, you're one as well. You weren't one bit mean today."

He wriggles his shoulders, like I'm sitting on them and he wants me gone. Like I'm the dumbest girl he ever came across. I walk with him as he wheels his bike around the corner, neither of us saying a word. When we're out of sight of Abe's place, I say, "See you."

He climbs on his bike and pedals away.

No sense bawling. Doesn't make you feel any better.

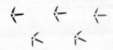

I head up the slope, watching for rocks, ferns swishing my knees. Ghost could be back in the barn right now, sitting on the rafters in the loft. So why I am scrambling over roots and boulders in search of a cat who'll run like a rabbit if he sees me?

Like most of my questions, I can't come up with an answer.

Unless it's because I'm a softie.

It's cooler in the trees. I circle behind Abe's barn. The hens are clustered in their outdoor pen, and from inside I hear hammering.

Ghost won't go near the barn with Abe making that much racket.

I walk deeper into the woods. I could do with a good gulp of iced tea right now; it feels like a lifetime ago, me and Davina sitting at her table.

Abe's face, the disappointment when he looked at me...how can I ever fix that?

I zigzag, my eyes flitting every which way in search of a patch of white. When I'm out of earshot of the hammering, I start calling Ghost's name, using my soft voice, the voice he's used to.

A flash of movement catches my eye.

Rabbit.

"Ghost," I call, "Ghost, where are you?"

The tops of the trees, the little gullies through the ferns and shrubs, the fallen trunks coated with moss, my eyes scout them all. I'm not wearing a watch. The sun's angling through the trees. Four-thirty? Five? If I'm late for supper, Seal will worry.

I've been climbing steady, and I'm pretty sure I'm in back of Ratchet. Maybe I should've gone to Gulley Cove first because Ghost used to live there.

If Ghost has vanished, Travis and Prinny will blame me.

I go faster, banging my knees on rocks, boughs slapping my face. The mosquitoes and blackflies are having a feast. I'm sweaty, thirsty, and tired, but it's like I can't stop from looking.

And then I see it. A patch of white. Between two trees. Not moving.

I rush forward, stoop, and push the boughs aside. Ghost. Ghost caught in a rabbit snare. Lying so still I'm sure he's dead.

With a whimper of distress, I lay my hand on his side. He gives this gasp, his eyes bulging. An old snare made of brass wire, rusty; whoever set it, must've forgotten it.

With all my strength, I yank the little metal post out of the ground. Using one finger, I loosen the loop that's cutting into Ghost's fur.

He shudders, his jaws gaping. After I loosen it some more, I ease it over his head. I pull off the shirt I'm wearing over my tank top, and wrap him in its soft folds. "It's okay, Ghost, it's okay. I'll take you to the vet and you'll be fine."

He's shivering now, his jaws still wide. I hurry through the woods, holding him close to my chest, talking to him the whole time, like that'll make him breathe normal.

I can't go to Abe's, and Travis's dad will still be at work. Maybe Davina is still home. If only I had my phone—I could text Lorne or Seal.

I come out behind the houses in Ratchet, right by Prinny's place. Her father has just turned into his driveway and he's climbing out of his truck. Relief makes my head swim. Hurrying past the new swing, I call, "Mr. Murphy! Please, can you take me to the vet?"

"Right now?" he says, scratching his head.

"A cat from Abe's barn, he got caught in a snare. *Please...*"

He opens the passenger door and helps me in. Then he walks around the hood, moving fast for a big man, gets in, and backs out the driveway.

"Thank you," I say. "He's not breathing right. I found him in the woods."

As he speeds up, I hold Ghost close. We're nearly at the clinic before he speaks again. "Prinny was after tellin' me you been mendin' your ways."

"Prinny said that?"

"I was right glad to hear it."

"Thanks," I mumble.

We arrive at the clinic five minutes before closing time. It's a different receptionist. She ushers us into a little room and Dr. Larkin, the vet, walks in fast, her red hair in a swirl around her head. I tell her my name and explain how I found Ghost. "He's one of Travis's feral cats. He lives in Abe's barn."

"Travis and Ghost have both been here before," she says, smiling at me.

Her hands move swift as she examines Ghost. He's breathing better now, although he's still shivering.

Gently she massages his chest. "Was he struggling when you found him?"

"No. Lying still. Like he was terrified. Or dead."

"Smart cat. Smarter than a rabbit. The snare didn't break his skin, so he couldn't have struggled much—sometimes an animal who's already been traumatized plays dead when there's a new threat...I'll give him a tranquilizer, to relax him. Will you take him home or back to the barn?"

I can't face Abe. "I'll take him home. But he's not very tame."

"I'll loan you a cat cage. Keep him in one room for a few days, Sigrid, even though he'll probably howl the place down. Then gradually give him the run of the house. Lots of petting, if he'll let you, and good quality food."

Prinny's father says, "I'll pay the bill, and buy the food and litter...Sigrid can pay me back when she's able."

My eyes fasten themselves on a glob of cat hair on the floor. I whisper, "That's real nice of you, Mr. Murphy."

We're about to leave, me horrified by how much one short visit to the vet costs, when Dr. Keating, Travis's dad, strides in the door. He's my doctor, and when I had an earache in February, he was as kind as could be.

No cage in his hand, no cat tucked under his arm. He smiles at Dr. Larkin, the sort of smile I figure Seal's giving Davina, and I remember the rumors I heard a while ago, that he and Dr. Larkin were dating. I can't imagine Travis being anything but happy if he ends up with Dr. Larkin as his stepmom.

We drive to Fiddlers Cove. Seal's truck is parked in our driveway. My bike, which Tate stole, is lying on the lawn. So you could say she just borrowed it.

It's way past suppertime.

Prinny's father carries the food and kitty litter to the front door, which he pushes open. Seal rushes out of the kitchen. "Sigrid! Where have you been? Are you all right?"

"I'm fine," I say. "Thank you, Mr. Murphy—I'll bring the money tomorrow."

By tomorrow the word will be out that Hud wrecked Abe's garden and let the cow loose and me not doing one thing to stop him.

Mr. Murphy nods at Seal, smiles at me, and off he goes.

You better remember that smile...won't be many coming your way from now on.

Quickly I explain to Seal how I found Ghost behind Abe's barn. I carry the cage into my bedroom. Seal brings a bowl of water, another bowl of cat pellets, and a big plastic pan that he fills with the litter. After I find an old blanket in the linen cupboard, I fold it to make a bed in the corner. Last, I open the latch on the cage.

Ghost blinks at me sleepily. I stroke him, head to tail, head to tail, his fur silkier than I expected, and hear Seal leave the room, shutting the door real quiet. I stay put, stroking and talking as gentle as I can, hoping so deep that when the tranquilizer wears off, Ghost will remember how my voice sounds and how my hand feels.

After a while, he falls asleep.

I close my bedroom door and go into the kitchen.

"Dinner's dried up by now," Seal says, and reaches for a spoon. "Lorne ate and left. He was worried, too, so I just called him to tell him you're okay."

It's Monday. The day I was supposed to be home to feed my brother.

Someone bangs on the door.

I jump like I'm Ghost.

Seal goes to the door. Abe says, "Your kid home, Seal? The girl?"

I want to die. Right here and right now.

TWENTY-SEVEN

to solve

Feet dragging, I walk into the living room. Seal's staring from me to Abe. "What's up?" he says.

My throat's so dry I can't talk. Through a haze of misery, I hear Abe say, "I owes you a big apology, Sigrid. You and your buddy, Hud."

"What?"

"It wasn't him. It was them two girls, just like you said, and I'll be goin' there next."

"But how—"

"Hud, didn't he go straight to Travis's place. Happens Travis saw two girls go past on bicycles. Recognized your bike. The girl on it, she had mud on her sneakers."

"Hud went to *Travis's?*"

"Next on, he and Travis went to Tate Cody's place and stole her sneakers, the ones with the mud on. They—"

"*Stole* them? How?"

He cackles. "Sneakers were dryin' on the step. Travis went up innocent as sunrise and tol' Tate her friend Mel had fallen off her bike up the road a ways. The two of 'em took off to find Mel—Tate wearin' sandals, Travis on his bike so he could make his getaway. Meantime, Hud snuck to the front door and done the stealin'."

Travis and Hud as a team? Hud hates Travis.

"They brung the sneakers to my place," Abe goes on, "and stuck 'em in the tracks in the garden. Perfect fit. Carrot tops and beet greens squashed in the soles. Travis was right angry I didn't believe you. Hud didn't say much but you could tell he wasn't happy. Maybe he ain't so bad after all. Sneakers are in the truck. Evidence."

I say, edgy-like, "So are you back to trusting me, Abe?"

"I'm right sorry I accused Hud of wreckin' my place and that I didn't listen to you. But you gotta admit it looked bad."

I have to say it. "If it hadn't been for me, Tate and Mel wouldn't have gone there."

"Wasn't you let Rosie out."

"I never would've done that! Nor would Hud."

He shuffles his feet in their rubber work boots. "I knows that now. You and him can come back any time and I trusts you, sure." He gives me a sly grin. "The pig was some happy to have ten minutes in the garden."

Wanting it all in the open, I tell Abe that Ghost is in my room. "Well, now," he says, "if the cat will settle, that's good by me."

I think of the barn, its rafters and mice, its door to the outside. "He might not settle. If not, can he come back?"

"Course he can."

"Will you leave Tate and Mel to me, Abe? When I'm done with them, they won't come near your place again."

"You're sure now?"

"I'm sure."

"Okay...but I'll hold onto them muddy sneakers just in case." He tips his ball cap. "I'm off, then. Gonna replant the beets and carrots tonight. Full moon, that'll help."

His old truck roars out the driveway. Seal looks at me. "Supper," he says. "And you better fill me in."

It takes a while because Seal wants all the details. When I'm finished, he says, *"Softie*...I think Hud means you're kind."

I duck my head. "I wasn't one bit kind when I was a Shrike."

"You're changing your ways," he says and carries the plates over to the counter. "Davina called, told me how you visited her and how much she liked you."

I blush with pleasure. "I like her, too."

He opens the dishwasher and pulls out the cutlery rack. "We're gonna get married, Sigrid. Once that happens, I figure your mother will stay home for a while, just like she did when I moved in. But it'll wear off. We know that, you and me."

Yeah, we know.

"So this week," he says, "I'll start building an extension on the back of Davina's place. Another bedroom and bathroom. For you. It's not a perfect solution, and likely there'll be difficulties along the way with your mother. But any time you want, you can stay with us. Stay as long as you like." He clears his throat. "You okay with that idea?"

I put the cloth down on the counter, wrap my arms around his waist, and hold on tight. My voice muffled by his shirt, I say, "Seal, you're my real dad."

He puts his arms around me. We stand there quite a while. Then I lift my head. "Guess I'll be buying another bedspread."

"And another soap dish."

Knowing you're happy makes you even happier.

TWENTY-EIGHT

to dance

Seal drives me to Prinny's place, where he insists on paying for the vet. We drop in on Davina for tea. She shows me the back of the house, and where they plan to add the two rooms. I hug her when we leave.

Ghost is stirring in his cage when we get home. I settle on the bed. A little later, he staggers out of the cage, drinks noisily, sniffs the kitty litter and squats in it, then wanders back to the cage.

At two in the morning, I wake up. *Eeeoouuw... eeeooouuuw...*

I talk to him softly, watching him prowl around the room, testing all the corners, peering under the bed. After he chomps on some food, he jumps on the bed, gives me a startled look, jumps down again, and disappears underneath it.

The wind ruffles my curtains. Figuring out that Seal is my real dad and that I'll always have a home with him and Davina—it's shifted stuff. My other dad said he liked my letters, so I'll keep writing them. But I'm going to start phoning him once a week. And I'm not planning to talk about the weather. He's gonna hear some real stuff, whether he likes it or not.

Who knows, I might fly out west and visit him. Him and his new family.

The other thing I'm going to do is phone Hanna. Confess how I've lied to her, how I was a Shrike for two years, with no other friends but Tate and Mel. Then I'll just have to hope she'll forgive me.

If she does, and if I flew to Fort McMurray, I could do a detour and visit her. Just the thought of it fills me with longing.

What a lot we'd have to talk about...

Next time I wake up, it's morning and Ghost is on the prowl again, wailing and moaning. I hate seeing him so restless and unhappy. Maybe the barn *is* the best place for him. He's used to freedom and space, with the pig and the hens for company.

On top of that, Tate lives two doors down from here. I'm not sure I'll ever really trust her. And what if Mel comes to visit...Mel, the champion rock-thrower. Then there's Davina. When I spend time at her place, Ghost will have two homes, two places to settle into.

I'll give it a few days, be as patient as I know how.

If I take him back to Abe's, is that called quitting?
Or is it being kind?

When I climb out of bed, Ghost streaks under it.

After breakfast, I check Tate's driveway. The car's gone. When I ring the bell, she opens the door, sees it's me, and tries to slam it shut. But my foot is stuck in the gap.

"Tate, you're never going near Abe's again, you or Mel. If you do, he'll tell your father and Mel's father what you both did yesterday. Destruction of property. Endangering livestock. Your father won't like that. Will he?"

"That's blackmail!"

"You're the expert."

She almost spits the words. "Don't give me orders."

"Abe has evidence. Your sneakers. With mud on them."

"So *that's* what happened to my sneakers—I knew Travis and Hud were trouble. Why didn't Abe tell on me?"

"I asked him not to."

"I see what you're up to—you want me jumping to your tune, don't you, Sigrid? Just like my parents want me jumping to theirs."

So much bitterness in her voice that my heart quails.

"All I want is for you and Mel to stay away from Abe's. And I'll tell on you if I have to."

I won't tell. Ever. But she doesn't have to know that.

"You got it all sewed up," she says.

I think of Ghost prowling and howling. I think of Mel and Carly Rae Jepsen, of Hud and Doyle. I think of Tate being forced to her knees.

"You know something, Tate? You don't smile often, not a real smile. But when you do, you look nice. You should do it more often."

She bares her teeth. "Like this?"

Then she bangs the door shut.

I'm scarcely home when there's a knock at the front door. For a crazy moment I wonder if Tate has changed her mind already.

Travis, Prinny, Laice, and Hector are lined up outside, their bikes littering the lawn. Prinny steps forward. "Thank you for looking after Ghost," she says, and gives me a smile, a smile that warms me clear to my toes.

"You're welcome," I say.

Travis says, "We're having a barbecue at my place tomorrow evening. Six o'clock. Can you come?"

"I'd love to," I say, my voice kind of wavering. "And thanks, Travis, for listening to Hud and for going with him to Tate's. Abe came by yesterday, and we're all straightened away."

He grins. "Me and Hud. What a concept."

Laice says, "You can tell us tomorrow how Ghost is getting along." More smiles.

"Yeah," says Hector, then he smiles.

I stand on the step watching them bike down the road. Happiness...I could get used to it.

Doyle's truck is in their driveway. I don't want to go anywhere near him because he'll recognize me as the girl who tripped him at Home Hardware.

Maybe Hud's sitting on his rock.

But when I reach Abe's place, Hud is at the top of the garden, digging up sods and tossing them in a pile. Abe's bent over his tiller, tinkering with the motor.

Rosie the cow is tethered in a patch of long grass back of the garden, chewing away. No sign of the pig.

I park my bike against the fence. Lucy runs at me, barking. Hud sees me and straightens, stretching his back as I walk closer.

Abe grins at me. "Got me a new helper," he says. "None too shabby."

Hud rolls his eyes. His t-shirt is streaked with mud and his workboots are caked with mud. But he looks good.

Relaxed, like Ghost on his tranquilizer.

"Can I help?" I ask.

"You can take them sods and carry 'em behind the barn to the manure pile," Abe says.

Hud offers me his bug spray. Then we all work away for an hour or more, Abe tilling the part Hud's cleared of sod. Abe's replanted his rows of carrots and beets, and Tate missed some of the potatoes and parsnips.

"Peas are a write-off," Abe says. "Weather too warm to replant."

He brings us glasses of water, cold from the well. Then he says, "Take a break, you two. Hud, if you wants to come back tomorrow morning, we could tackle the woodpile."

"Okay," Hud says.

Then him and me bike to his rock, where we sit for a while, gazing at the horizon. Hud says, "Abe's paying me to work for him." He picks at a hole in his jeans with his dirty fingernails. "I used to throw rocks at Lucy."

"I used to frighten kids so they'd give us money."

I pull my eyes away from the horizon and fasten them on Hud. "Abe came to our place last night and apologized. If you hadn't gone to see Travis and stolen the sneakers... if Abe still thought you ruined his barn and garden while I stood by watching...that would've been so awful, I don't know how I could've stood it. Thanks, Hud. You were right kind."

"A softie?"

"Kind."

"It was wrong, us getting blamed for something we didn't do."

"Like your dad, who blames you for everything?"

"Yeah..." He picks at the hole some more. "Next time he lays into me with his fists, I'm going to the cops."

My jaw drops. "When did you decide that?"

"Yesterday afternoon—he wanted to know where I'd been and I wouldn't tell him, so he belted me one."

"Did you warn him you'd go to the cops?"

He shrinks a little. "No sense tipping him off beforehand."

"Travis, Hector, and me, we've all seen your dad hit you. And we'd all go with you as witnesses."

"You *would?*"

"You bet."

"All of you? No kidding?"

"The last few days, I've been asking around. Hector and Travis are the only ones who've actually seen your dad hit you."

"Oh," Hud says. "Thanks."

"Seal will keep his eyes open, too."

Hud says hoarsely, "It was because of you—you trying to quit being a Shrike and not getting anywheres, Mel and Tate being so mean, I dunno, Sigrid, somehow it all went together and I knew I had to do something."

He grabs my hand, which is as dirty as his, and clutches it, staring out to sea.

"*Mean*...it won't win, Hud."

"I hope not." Hud shivers. "He'll be some mad."

"You and your sister, you can come to our place any time you need to. Seal's the best kind and he wouldn't take any guff off your dad."

The horizon is as sharp as the edge of a sword. Hud's not leaning into it, though. He's sitting on a rock, a good solid rock, and he's still holding my hand.

He says, "Thought I'd go into town for a donair. Want to come?"

"I'd like that...I'll have to check on Ghost on the way."

Hud stands in the doorway of my room and watches me scoop the kitty litter and fill the food bowl. Ghost is on top of my bureau, his tail whipping back and forth.

As we leave, Hud says, so low I can scarce hear, "See ya, Ghost."

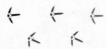

By four o'clock I'm home and Hud's on his way to his place. I fiddle with Lorne's boom box until I find a disco station, and take my socks off. I turn the volume up and start to dance, kind of stiff at first, then looser, until the rhythm takes me over and the beat pulses in my blood.

Just me and the music, dancing.

THE NINE LIVES OF TRAVIS KEATING

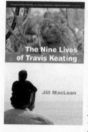

After his mother's death, Travis Keating and his father move to Ratchet, Newfoundland, to start a new life. Some life. Travis soon discovers that only a few oddballs show any interest in him: Cole, a talker who soon makes himself scarce; Hector, a strange kid whose ears stick out; and Prinny, a girl as scraggly as her skinny ponytail. Nobody you can really call a friend. And then there's Hud, the toughest, nastiest bully in school, who hates "townies" and promises to make Travis's life an utter misery. But Travis doesn't care. He's got his "funeral face," a tight mask that gives away nothing and allows him to hide his feelings. Funeral face comes in handy, especially with parents and other adults who think they know what you're feeling every minute of the day.

But funeral face can also make him reckless, and Travis decides to visit the dangerous Gulley Cove, with its treacherous wharf and its tumbledown fish shacks, which some of the kids say are haunted. Instead of ghosts, Travis discovers a colony of feral cats, sickly and starving, and unused to kindness. Putting aside his own problems to care for them is about to bring Travis more satisfaction—and more danger—than he ever would have thought possible.

A stunning first children's novel, *The Nine Lives of Travis Keating* is a moving story about coping with grief. But more than that, it's about belonging, learning to be a friend, and finding bravery in the most unexpected of places.

Reviews

"*The Nine Lives of Travis Keating*, is a fast and engaging read... MacLean is to be congratulated on a marvelous achievement. Highly Recommended."
—*CM Magazine*

"Jill MacLean gently beckons readers into this small Newfoundland village as she delicately captures a true sense of the place and its people. She beautifully depicts the wide range of emotions that often threaten to overcome Travis."
—*Atlantic Books Today*

"Travis is likeable and sympathetic...a boy of imagination, courage, and empathy. This is a solid piece of contemporary fiction with an interesting story."
—*School Library Journal*

Awards

Ann Connor Brimer Award for Children's Literature Winner, 2009

On the International Board on Books for Young People (IBBY) Honour List

On Resource Link's "Best of 2008" List

CLA Children's Book of the Year Award shortlist, 2009

2009 KIND Children's Honor Book

Canadian Children's Book Centre Our Choice, 2009—Starred Choice

OLA's Silver Birch Fiction nominee 2010

Rocky Mountain Book Award Shortlist, 2011

Pennsylvania School Library Association Top 40 Fiction, 2009

The Present Tense of Prinny Murphy

The Present Tense of Prinny Murphy picks up the story where *The Nine Lives of Travis Keating* leaves off—but this time, from the perspective of Prinny, Travis's friend.

An alcoholic mother, a distracted father, a best friend who spends all his time with his new "girlfriend," and three relentless schoolyard bullies: Prinny Murphy's past, present, and future certainly are "tense".

Adding to her misery, she still can't read well enough to escape from remedial lessons with the dour Mrs. Dooks. But when a kindly substitute teacher introduces her to LaVaughn's inner-city world in the free verse novel, *Make Lemonade*, Prinny discovers that life can be full of possibilities—and poetry.

Reviews

"Jill MacLean's *The Present Tense of Prinny Murphy* is a moving, engaging, troublesome book that middle school readers will find difficult to put down. *The Present Tense of Prinny Murphy* is the sequel to the 2008 novel, *The Nine Lives of Travis Keating*. As good as the first book was, the second instalment is even better. As hard-hitting as the first book was, the second one hits much harder. While the same characters continue to face many of the same problems, MacLean's writing remains fresh and engaging. Issues of bullying, family secrets, alcoholism, loneliness, and child abuse again form much of the framework for her novel and MacLean again handles these issues in a sensitive, skilful manner that at once is interesting and informative.
Highly Recommended."
—*CM Magazine*

"Beautifully layered and sensitively written."
—*Quill & Quire*

"The characters are multidimensional and believable. All of them have flaws and secrets balanced with flashes of goodness. MacLean weaves (the characters) into a raw, realistic novel that reminds readers that finding your voice is sometimes harder than using it."
—*School Library Journal*

"In this beautifully engaging book, Prinny, about 12, has much to deal with...The exotic northern setting is carefully depicted and plays a major role in both mood and plot. As Prinny learns effective ways to deal with the truly evil, completely believable Shrikes with too little adult support, readers may pick up a point or two. Although this is a sequel (*The Nine Lives of Travis Keating*, 2009) it out-stands alone perfectly."
—*Kirkus*

Awards

Ann Connor Brimer Award for Children's Literature Winner, 2010

On the 2011 USBBY Outstanding International Books honor list

2010 Ruth and Sylvia Schwartz Children's Book Award Nominee

On Resource Links Best Books of 2009 list

2010 OLA Best Bets—Children's Fiction

Canadian Library Association Book of the Year for Children Award 2011

On VOYA's Top Shelf Fiction for Middle School Readers 2010 list